BLIND POOL

PRAISE FOR BLIND WITNESS

A 'spiffingly' good murder mystery story set in the 1920's

- **Eve Bonham** author of *Dear Magpies*

Funny and charming, this novel is well worth reading.

- **Gail Aldwin** author of *The String Games*

This is a wonderful, readable, exciting and highly desirable book! I have many books to read, but this one kept luring me back.

- **northernreader** (professional reviewer)

It is so very difficult to get a niche in the market to make a book stand out from the rest and well Vicki Goldie seems to have done that.

- **Susan Hampson** Top 1000 Reviewer Amazon

BLIND POOL

Vicki Goldie

First published in Great Britain in 2020 by
Victorina Press
Wanfield Hall
Kingstone
Uttoxeter
Staffordshire, ST14 8QR
England

Typesetting and Layout: Jorge Vasquez
Cover design © Fiona Zechmeister

British Library Cataloguing in Publication Data
A catalogue record for this book is available from the British Library.

ISBN: 978-1-8380360-2-7

Typeset in 12pt Garamond
Printed and bound in Great Britain by 4edge ltd.

DEDICATION

To Rosalind Hand,
former Senior Sister at Poole Hospital Emergency Department,
gone but not forgotten.

THE CHARTERS' MYSTERIES SERIES

This series follows amateur sleuths Major Alasdair Charters and the Honourable Melissa Charters as they inadvertently muddle their way through many investigations but always arrive at the truth. Alasdair was blinded in the First World War and uses his special skills to gain 'insight' into the crimes. The Honourable Melissa, who likes to think she is a socialist, has a large family and set of friends who always seem to run into problems. The books are set both in England and abroad.

Having a husband who is blind, author Vicki Goldie likes to explore perceptions about this disability and push the boundaries.

MELISSA'S LIST

Family

1. Colonel William Gauntlet
2. Marjorie Gauntlet – wife of William Gauntlet
3. Davinia Gauntlet – daughter of William Gauntlet
4. Charles Gauntlet – son of William Gauntlet
5. Serena Gauntlet – wife of Charles Gauntlet
6. Robert and Lucy Gauntlet – children of above
7. Major Roderick Gauntlet – cousin of Colonel Gauntlet
8. Great Aunt Petunia – mother of Roderick Gauntlet
9. Lavender Gauntlet (deceased) – mother of William Gauntlet and sister of Petunia
10. Hazel Richards – nanny/governess

Below stairs

1. Butler – Dobson
2. Housekeeper – Bertha Dobson
3. Housemaids – Elsie and Betsy
4. Chef – Raoul Dufour
5. Kitchen maid – Flora
6. Chauffeur/ Handyman – Frank Dunmore

House guests

1. Major Alasdair Charters
2. The Honourable Melissa Charters – friend of Davinia Gauntlet
3. Captain Arthur Searle – friend of William and Marjorie Gauntlet
4. Elizabeth Searle – friend of William and

Marjorie Gauntlet

5. Sheridan Kennard – Financial consultant from the USA
6. Rosalind Foote – District nurse

Pennstone Manor

1. Brigadier and Lady Honor Ferguson
2. Davies – the estate manager
3. Thomas – Alasdair Charters' valet

PROLOGUE

The skulls grinned up at him, floating and bobbing like apples at Halloween. Heart pounding to the sound of the guns, he sat up, wiping the chill sweat from his face. A damn flashback from the war. A shell hole filled with water, the mud slipping and sucking at his feet, threatening to draw him into oblivion in the dark pool. Why now? Would he never be free? He sighed, stilling his breathing. Why on earth had they started again, the flashbacks, the nightmares? Was it the strange house? The water? Or the murder?

ONE

1923
SOMEWHERE IN DORSET

'This compartment smells rather frowsty. Are you sure it is first class?' He put a hand out to steady himself as a gust of wind buffeted the carriage from side to side.

'It most certainly is, Alasdair, darling. Credit me with some sense.'

He winced as Melissa dug him in the ribs, and he took her hand in the hope of restraining any more excesses. She forgot sometimes that he could not anticipate such moves and tense his muscles in expectation. As a result, all boisterous thumps into soft flesh hurt.

'Well, I thought they had bought new rolling stock? I was expecting a little more comfort than this. Ugh, even the seats are sticky.' He withdrew his hand and rubbed it on his tweed trousers, hoping his wife hadn't noticed. Since they had moved to the New Forest, he seemed to live in tweeds. Melissa had told him the attire was just the ticket for the few days they were spending in Somerset. He wondered what his wonderful wife was wearing. Tweeds too and fashionable low-heeled brogues? He hoped she had brought some of her flapper evening dresses. He like the tactile feeling of the fabrics.

'Perhaps they heard about the storms and put on an old one instead?' Melissa suggested.

Another gust of wind rattled the windows of the compartment and a stray branch hit the window, making them both jump.

'Good grief, Alasdair, that branch is stuck there despite the speed of the train. Completely obscuring the view, such as it was. And Dorset is so beautiful normally, so rural, so empty. Now all I can see are thick sheets of rain and not the landscape. What a shame.'

All Alasdair could think of was how the dampness heightened the fusty smell on this popular line into the West Country – a train that would have been full in the summer months as people escaped to the seaside. Today it was virtually empty. They'd had no problem in gaining a compartment to themselves, even with the dog. He bent down and patted the head of Sheba, his guiding retriever, sitting at his feet unperturbed by the storm raging outside.

Melissa had brought a picnic prepared by Mrs Smithers, the cook: lovely ham sandwiches, slices of cake, a Thermos of tea and, joy of joys, champagne. While eating the delicate sandwiches – crusts off – he contemplated his good fortune in having an organised wife and a superb cook. Of course, she was really the Brigadier and Lady Honor's cook, and despite them telling him the estate was his to manage, he had changed none of the staff as they were so good.

'Did you manage to escape most of the deluge?' he asked. 'It was coming down pretty hard at the last change.'

'Oh yes, the Warm coat has absorbed most of it, as did yours. My cloche hat saved most of my hair.'

He could just imagine her, the hat tossed onto the

seat, her long fingers fluffing her blonde curls: an image that filled him with regret that he could no longer see her in the flesh. He wished she had not moved to sit opposite him; that was easier to serve the picnic, he surmised. He would have liked to ruffle her hair and make contact. This was not going to be an easy weekend. They might have come through the murders at Pennstone Manor last year, but that did not mean he wanted to repeat the experience. He paused for a moment, with a particularly luscious slice of coffee walnut cake still half eaten in his hand, listening to the clickety clack of the train on the tracks. The carriage shook again and he was suddenly convinced he was breathing in smuts, the sharp, burnt coal smell overtaking that of the cake.

'Is the window open? I'm sure I am covered smuts,' he complained.

'No, it isn't. Silly. You would have felt the draught if it was. I think it's the movement of the carriage and it being so old and smelly. The air is not particularly salubrious in here. And the branch is still there.'

He took a large bite out of the slice of the cake. It melted in his mouth and quite dispelled the taste of coal. He smiled then frowned. 'Have we slowed down?' he muttered. 'Do you think we will be on time?'

He heard Melissa sigh. He knew he was being a pain, but it was so difficult journeying without sight and then worrying about their time away. He just hoped their hosts would send a comfortable motor to pick them up when they got there. It was still some twenty-five miles to their intended destination from the station. Home to the Gauntlets, Chudley House was nestled within the Somerset Levels, an atmospheric area prone to mist and fog, he recalled.

'Sorry, darling, I am sure we have not slowed down. If anything, it seems more frenetic. We are certainly being thrown about. I have just spilled champagne in my lap.'

He heard her leap up and the sound of brushing as she flicked the champagne off her skirt. He took the opportunity to lean forward and pull her into him. Yes, tweed skirt and cashmere sweater. Very nice: warm, practical and delightfully rounded in the right places. She giggled and then kissed the top of his head. He was glad she had not patted it; he was not the dog. Realising his nerves were creeping in dangerously, he searched for distraction.

'So who can we expect this weekend then?' he asked.

'Well, the Gauntlets are rather a large clan. Davinia is single – she lost her fiancé in the war. So sad and she has never met anyone else. I am not sure if that is from choice or bad luck. Of course, she is much older than me, but she did a lot of hospital visiting as I did in the war. We met travelling to London and hit it off.'

'I am lucky, aren't I?' She leant over and kissed his cheek, dancing out of his way as he moved to pull her to him again. Or pulled by the motion of the carriage, he could not tell. As a former spy it worried him, these gaps in his knowledge. It was in the small lacunae that mistakes crept in. And with mistakes came vulnerability.

'Let me see.' Melissa seemed unaware of his mood swing and continued on. 'There is Colonel William Gauntlet. He hasn't fought since he was in India but that doesn't stop him pulling rank, apparently.'

'True, but I guess they may want to emphasise they

did their bit and survived. So many didn't.'

'Yes, you are right, but you don't call yourself "Major", do you?'

'Only when I need a table somewhere, but then your Honourable is jolly useful for that too,' he teased, humour restored.

'Urgh, I loathe it. It just impresses all the worst kind of people and puts the back up of those who might be sympathetic and likeminded friends.'

'Darling, don't tell me you yearn to be middle class. Your grandfather would have your guts for garters, and I don't think your father would be best pleased.'

'Well, it was OK for them – they had grand titles and estates to match. I am not sure it benefits the rest of us much. A pure affectation, if you ask me, and I am happy to drop it.'

'Who else will be there?' Alasdair was anxious to forestall a socialist lecture. Melissa had been a big fan of Keir Hardie and was reserving her judgement on Ramsay MacDonald. It could be hard work.

'There is this cousin, Major Roderick Gauntlet, who has recently come to live with them. I wonder if he hates being a lower rank?' She laughed. 'I gained the impression that Davinia was not happy about this situation. Davinia's mother, Marjorie, is alive and well, no doubt running things in regimental fashion. Oh, and there is some ancient great aunt with the improbable name of Petunia, can you imagine?'

Sadly, Alasdair could, only too well. 'Anyone else?'

'Yes, there is Charles Gauntlet, son and heir, and his wife, Serena. They have two children, a boy and a girl, I think. I suppose there will be a governess or nanny or some such as well.'

'How on earth did you ferret out all this information? Surely not just from one letter?'

'Hah, no, Aunt Honor's jungle drums. There is some sort of mystery or scandal surrounding the Uncle Roderick – he arrived from South Africa recently, I have been led to believe. He actually is the son of Aunt Petunia. Weird, what?'

'Well done, Aunt Honor. I am so glad it has worked, splitting the house and us moving in. They both have such good contacts. Invaluable for sleuthing. Should we wish to continue?' He raised an eyebrow.

'Oh, they are both an information goldmine,' Melissa agreed. 'And so keen to share it.' She laughed again. 'And yes, we do.'

'The Gauntlets certainly believe in family living if Aunt Honor's information is correct. Rather sweet, really, all those generations in one house. It must be huge. Another nightmare for me to navigate, I suppose.' Would he ever be able to relax? He hated being such a burden and knew that most of the effort would land on Melissa. How did she put up with him? Remembering the socialism, he decided to reserve judgement. Thank goodness for Sheba, he thought. She was really coming on. From failed gun dog to a blind man's helper, all their training together was helping them both, he was convinced.

'There is one thing, though. Davinia said that until recently her grandmother lived there as well but she died a very short time ago.'

TWO

FRIDAY AFTERNOON

The train conductor tapped on the door of the compartment and called out that their station was the next stop.

The train pulled into a typical rural south-west station. Not that much could be seen, as the darkness, punctuated by the rain falling in stair rods, obscured any finer details. Melissa stood up by the door to the platform and it was immediately seized and opened by the stationmaster, enveloped in a flapping sou'wester.

'Hurry now. The water's rising. The train needs to be in Devon tonight.' His voice was gruff but worried.

Melissa was grateful to spy Thomas, Alasdair's valet, coming down the platform, followed by a porter. She handed down to him her small valise and the picnic basket and then hopped onto the platform. She turned and made to guide Alasdair out of the train. However, Sheba had already stepped down and Alasdair had followed. She grimaced; she was not at all sure about his faith in the dog. He seemed to have developed almost a recklessness over the last year, letting Sheba lead him into situations Melissa frankly found hair-raising. He had gone from total dependence on her to a form of independence with the dog. Thrilled as she wanted to be with this way forward, she watched and waited in silence and could not stop herself worrying all the same. She looped his arm around hers and they then dashed for cover into the ticket office and waiting room.

'Phew.' Alasdair shook himself like a dog. 'I hope they have decent transport. It is still a way to go.'

'A Bentley,' came Thomas's laconic reply, but he added, 'Room for all of us, although the luggage will get wet.'

The chauffeur of the magnificent car helped Thomas with the luggage, his face anxious, his movements almost frenetic. The larger cases were covered in oilcloth and lashed to the back of the car. Melissa crossed her fingers for her evening dresses. The picnic basket went on the roof. With Thomas in the front with the chauffeur, Alasdair and Melissa had room in the back between them for two small valises. At least their overnight things would not arrive damp. With all the leg room available in what seemed a vast car, Sheba rested quietly at Alasdair's feet. The lead slung loosely across his knees.

The chauffeur seemed in a terrific hurry, the tyres crunching on the loose gravel as they set off. 'The water is rising,' he shouted. 'We need to be over the bridge beyond the village in the next half hour or we may not make it.' He sounded anxious.

Melissa turned to Alasdair and raised her eyebrows. Then remembered, as she so often did, especially at moments of tension or excitement, that such gestures were wasted on him.

'What do you mean?' she called back. The wind had not abated and the car did little to muffle the tumult.

'It's the Levels. Going to be a bad one this year. You mark my words.' He sounded like a prophet of doom.

Melissa sighed. Was this going to be another disastrous weekend in the country? Why were they always asked away in the autumn or winter? What happened to summer cocktails on the lawn? Tennis? Then she glanced at her husband and realised with a pang that he would hate it. That was why they were going now. They had spent all the last year preparing their new accommodation at Pennstone Manor, and there had been drinks on the lawn, when he had learned to find it. With his face in repose, she realised he was tired. Faint lines were crinkling around his eyes even though he was only twenty-seven. Heavens, in three years he would be thirty. Positively ancient.

She resisted the urge to look in her compact mirror to check her own features. Alasdair turned his head as if his eyes were seeking hers. She reached over the cases and squeezed his shoulder. He might have his demons, but he was here safe, not buried in a field in Flanders.

He smiled a response. 'What on earth is going on?' he shouted, 'What is that noise?'

'The storm, I think, the wind, the rain and the tyres. I do not think this is going to be a relaxed journey!'

The chauffeur, whose name, it transpired after much shouting back and forth, was Dunmore, drove at speed with no concession for bends or indeed any other traffic that might be on the narrow country roads. It was as if he knew they would be alone on the road this late afternoon, and it was as if the devil chased them. They sped along the road, which was heavy with water; the noise of the tyres and the resulting spray was so bad that conversation was impossible. As it was dark, the spray also obscured any vision either side, which would have been limited anyway given the height of the hedges. Every so often the car juddered, and she saw that Alasdair kept being pitched about as he could not anticipate the movement. She shouted to him the location of the door strap, as she feared his nose might hit the screen between them and the front. Her side was partially open, but it could not be said that it was useful given the noise from outside.

'The bridge approaches. Hold on,' Dunmore shouted.

Melissa could see nothing other than the spray from the wheels and the almost overwhelming sound of running water. She hung onto the leather door strap for safety and attempted to peer through the open glass and out of the front windscreen. Impossible to see. She looked again out of the side window. The back of the car began to fishtail but then he got it back under control. She saw some startled white faces of men clutching sandbags caught in the headlamps and then the car was up a slope and at the top of the bridge. Looking down, it was impossible to say it was a bridge. The river was almost level with the road – the only thing keeping it back was the bridge walls. Then they were over and moving fast through standing water on the road, the car slewing a little, the sound jarring momentarily. Melissa sought Alasdair's hand as once more the spray kicking up either side gave her a fright.

'Will it hold?' she shouted, fighting panic.

'God willing,' came the gruff response from the front, the West Country burr suddenly prominent.

THREE

Within about three quarters of an hour, Dunmore had turned though a pair of imposing high-pillared gates with something in pale stone carved on top. Gargoyles? Eagles? They drove too fast for Melissa to see.

The drive was long and steep as they motored upwards to the house, perched like a large gothic monstrosity on a steep rise, punctured by lights on different levels. The car pulled onto the shingled forecourt in front of the house, the gravel grating under the wheels. They were obviously expected as the darkness was suddenly flooded by light as the front door opened and a butler and two female servants ran out holding enormous black umbrellas, buffeting in the wind so that they appeared to be huge black birds of ill omen swooping to collect them.

Melissa got out of the car, shivered and looked around. A maid had plucked Alasdair from the car and was propelling him into the house. She ran quickly behind; Alasdair hated to be manhandled. She was grateful now for the shelter of the umbrella. With a swift smile at the maid, she banished her momentary collywobbles. Entering the front porch the size of a room, she questioned her sanity in agreeing to this weekend. The house was enormous, far bigger than Pennstone Manor, where they now lived and shared with her aunt and uncle.

Once into the hall the darkness dissipated. Wide, bright and welcoming, a fire roaring in the grate. She caught up with Alasdair. He was bent over, fumbling for Sheba's lead. She grasped his hand and led him to the warmth of the fire. Then she stepped aside and glanced up at him. He had pulled off his hat. Even with the wide brim his hair was damp and curling. Looking at him sideways with his still evident military stance, she was for a moment able to admire him. Seeing him in that moment, no one could possibly tell that he was blind. He was a tall, slim, rather sleek man, but there was an air about him, a poise, as though he held himself coiled constantly ready for action. It must be exhausting. Even with the dog, this private, protected part of him had not dissipated over the year.

'Phew, that was hairy. Ride of the Valkyries or what?' He grinned.

'Definitely. Still, he was a good driver.'

The butler divested them of their hat and coats.

'So what is this about water rising?' Alasdair sounded suspicious.

'No idea. We will have to ask Davinia.' She was grateful he could not see her fingers crossed for luck.

As if summoned by her name, a rather beautiful woman came through one of the doors into the hall. She had enormous dove-grey eyes, eyes that ought to have been arresting, but she had such a worried expression on her face that they took on the impression of a wounded saint.

'Oh, I am so pleased you arrived safely. I dithered too long over the weather and then it was too late. We often get flooding down here, but there were dire warnings this time. It is so hard to know whether to credit country folk, isn't it?'

She had a lovely husky voice, slightly breathy, that in another might seem affected, but it suited her. Melissa remembered it had been put to good use in their hospital visiting during the war. Davinia had read well, acting out all the parts like a professional actress.

She approached Alasdair and took both his hands in hers. 'You must be Alasdair, so pleased to meet you. I have heard so much about your exploits.' She ducked her head to one side of him to catch Melissa's eye. An impish grin lit her features and she gave an exaggerated wink.

Melissa chuckled; Davinia had been great fun.

'And this must be your working dog. Melissa has told me about it. The dog will have full range of the house. I have arranged it. May I touch it?'

Alasdair was warmed that she asked and didn't assume. He smiled. 'Meet Sheba, the most intelligent retriever in the country.'

Davinia stroked the silky head, her eyes sparkling with some amusement. 'But I mustn't keep you standing here. You must be damp and frozen. Now we can have tea in the drawing room or whisky and soda in the library?'

Melissa became aware that Davinia was still holding Alasdair's hands. Perhaps something in her manner alerted Davinia and she dropped them with a faint shake of her head.

'I think I'd like something hot if you don't mind, but a whisky would be rather nice too. Is that rather greedy of me?' Melissa asked, distracted by the fleeting emotions that assailed her.

'How about milky coffee with a whisky on the side? Come on, let's go into the library, less chance of being disturbed there.' She spoke to the butler in an undertone and then led the way to a heavy wooden door that barely seemed to break up the dark wood panelling.

Melissa took Alasdair's hand; he raised his eyebrows at her and she squeezed his arm. Something was afoot.

Wonderfully, the library was warm. A large log fire burned in an open grate, the logs spitting and hissing as they released their air. Or was it the rain coming down the chimney? She guided him over to a leather Chesterfield sofa at an angle to the fire. The room was dark, almost sombre. Several lamps on tables were lit but barely pierced the gloom.

Davinia sat opposite them in a matching chair. She sighed, resting one hand on her chest. Leaning forward, her face reflected in light and shadows from the fire, her husky voice was intense. 'Look, I need to say this quickly or I may stop believing it myself. I think my grandmother was murdered, and I am very afraid I may be next.'

FOUR

There was a pause as the butler entered the room, his footsteps heavy and measured on the wood flooring. Davinia thanked him and then Alasdair felt a cool glass pushed against his right hand. He took it gratefully and lifted the glass, savouring the smell of the whisky – not a malt but it still smelled welcome after their journey. He took a huge gulp, the fire trailing down his throat bringing him back to attention. He waited for the sound of the door closing after the butler.

'So, tell me why you think your grandmother was murdered.'

'It is just a feeling, really. No, no, I know what you are going to say – it is all my imagination. Doctor Haymes signed the death certificate happily. He wouldn't listen to me and said I was imagining things, but I wasn't, I know I wasn't.' She sighed, a great shuddering noise. 'All right, let me get you settled in. Enjoy a lovely supper this evening and I will try and get my thoughts in order and tell you all about it in the morning.'

'Before we go, just tell me what the doctor said she died of,' Alasdair said.

'Gastritis and old age.'

'Well that can cover a multitude of stomach complaints, I believe. How old was she?'

'Just coming up to eighty-two.'

'A good age. I can see why he might consider old age

as a factor.'

'But she was bright as a button, really she was.'

'Well, let us have a quiet evening. Introduce us to the household and then we can see.'

'The household?' Davinia sounded confused.

'You haven't really thought this through, have you, Davinia?' Melissa said quietly. 'If you are, for example, thinking of poison, then it follows it was probably one of the household.'

'Random strangers rarely poison old ladies,' Alasdair's dry voice added gently.

'Oh yes, well, I see. You can discount the servants, but I believe we definitely have a murderer in the house. You solved the one at Pennstone Manor and I want you to do the same here.' Davinia was beginning to sound truculent.

'If we can, but are you prepared, whatever the consequences? It could be dangerous and extremely unpleasant,' Melissa said.

Alasdair grimaced on hearing the pain in her voice. It had not been easy finding the murderer in their home, and he was not sure the family would ever recover. 'However, let us not run before we can walk. There may be nothing here, and I promise you – whatever we do find or don't, we will be diligent.'

'That is all I want to know. I need peace of mind. Come, let me show you to your room.'

Alasdair stood, Sheba's lead in his right hand, and Melissa tucked his left around her arm.

Davinia had moved more quickly and threw open the door. 'Ha, Great Aunt Petunia, what a surprise. Were you looking for me? Let me introduce you. Major and the Honourable Mrs Charters, meet Great Aunt Petunia Gauntlet,' Davinia said wryly, a touch of humour in her voice.

There was a sniff in reply and footsteps moved away.

Melissa gave a hiccup, which could have been a supressed laugh, and squeezed his hand.

Alasdair grinned at her, awaiting her insights, and allowed her to lead him across an open space then up a staircase. Deep, wide treads, twenty-five of them. Along a landing, up another two steps, and then into a room on the right.

'The bathroom is through that door there. I have jiggled the room arrangements around, so you will not be sharing the facilities.'

'Oh, that is kind.' Melissa sounded positively sunny; the room must be nice. 'Golly and Thomas has already unpacked your valises, Alasdair. How spiffing.'

'The first gong will be at six-thirty. We dine early here. Dinner at seven-thirty prompt. Daddy is very regimental.' Davinia sounded apologetic. 'Well, I'll leave you to settle in.' He heard the door close. 'And I'll send up some tea.'

'Phew.' Melissa sighed. 'What would you like to do first?' She let go of his arm.

'Well, how cluttered is the room?' Flipping up the lid of his Braille watch and feeling for the time, he added, 'We have just over an hour.'

They spent fifteen minutes pacing the room, clearing pathways to the bathroom and door. Melissa had become an expert on descriptions. 'I'll just move these bits out of the way,' she said as she lifted a couple of knickknacks and a flower display onto a high cabinet from a small circular table with two chairs stuck next to the dressing table. A positive obstacle course for a blind man. Then if Alasdair did bump into it, there was no harm done, other than more bruises to his legs.

There was a tap at the door. Melissa opened it to let in a housemaid in a positively Victorian uniform with a tray with tea and biscuits. Her dress had been badly taken up to a more modern length, but it was hideously out of date.

'Will you need a hand with dressing later, madam?' She didn't sound very enthusiastic.

'Not at all. I can manage. If there is a problem, I can ring?'

'The bell pull, madam.'

'Thank you, um?'

'Elsie, madam.' She gave a small attempt at a bob curtsey.

Positively antediluvian, thought Melissa. Surely not with Davinia's approval. She thought back to a few of the tussles she had been having at home with her Aunt Honor over the servant 'problem' at Pennstone Manor in the past year. Honor usually won as she was the one with experience of managing servants, but Melissa chipped away at entrenched attitudes whenever she could. She preferred to call them domestic staff. Their problem – if it could be called a problem – was that they were wealthy and could afford to pay good wages. Elsewhere, like here, it appeared, if there was no local competition for jobs, servants could be exploited. She remained keen on suffragism, but before she could lapse into another enthusiasm, she realised that poor Elsie was still waiting. Melissa smiled and muttered a quick, 'Thank you, Elsie.'

Melissa poured them tea and shared the biscuits; there was no telling what they would be eating for dinner. These Saturday to Monday visits, as they were sometimes termed, were not always run on the strictest of lines. However, in this military household, she rather suspected they were.

All their clothes had been hung and put away, except for Alasdair's evening clothes. She went to the wardrobe. His clothes were neatly ranged on the left, her things on the right. She already knew what she wanted to wear: a simple black sheath dress with black beading and lace. It was a little sombre, but she wanted to gauge the other guests before she launched her cocktail dresses on them. She suspected they were a little behind the times here in deepest Somerset.

Bathed, dressed and ready for the fray, they descended the stairs just as the first gong sounded. The butler turned, still with the striker in his hand, and with a nod of approval escorted them to a room leading off the great hall. From within, querulous voices could be heard. By the slight stiffening of his spine and his white knuckles from clutching Sheba's lead, Melissa could tell Alasdair was preparing himself. In apprehension or anticipation?

FIVE

FRIDAY COCKTAILS

The large room gave the overall impression of clutter and fullness. Not only because it appeared to be full of people but also, to Alasdair, because the room felt dense. Almost claustrophobic.

'Phew, I thought we would be early but the place is packed,' muttered Melissa, her tension communicating itself to Alasdair down her arm.

He could feel the tension radiating around the room; the conversation and raised voices had stopped as they entered.

'Oh good, you found us. We were just having a discussion about the moat.' Davinia had jumped up from her chair and came rapidly towards them, her footsteps making a sharp staccato across the floor, even on the rug.

Something had agitated her, thought Alasdair.

'The moat!' Melissa exclaimed.

'Well, that is what we call it. A bit of an exaggeration – it is really a deep ditch, but it's there to help keep the excess water under control. It has been a bit neglected over the years, though.'

'Yes, well,' a sharp voice with a trace of a colonial accent interrupted, 'I still can't see the panic. Surely this house is high enough. Even if, and I mean if, the rivers burst we will be fine.'

'Ah, Melissa and Alasdair, let me introduce my uncle, Major Roderick Gauntlet.'

Alasdair raised his eyebrows; suddenly they were informal with her uncle, and yet with Great Aunt Petunia their full honorifics had been used by Davinia. Was it because she had suspected her great aunt of eavesdropping or was she more relaxed with her uncle?

'Call me Roddy, everyone does, no point sticking to ceremony. Been retired for years.' There was something unctuous in his informality that set Alasdair on edge.

'Oh, I quite agree, Alasdair here is a major too, you know,' murmured Melissa. She winced and Alasdair wondered what had happened. Then his hand was firmly clasped and wrung.

'Well, you young whippersnappers had all the opportunities in the last show. Fighting on the velt was no fun, I can tell you.'

It was Alasdair's turn to tense. He could feel his right hand instinctively curling into a fist. If he could have seen him, he would have been hard pressed not to thump the old boy. He found it hard to believe that Davinia, whose fiancé was killed in the Great War, could possibly stomach this ribaldry. Under control, he asked lightly, 'Boer War?'

'Now that was real fighting, heat, dust and an uncivilised enemy who didn't recognise proper warfare.'

'Really, Roderick, that is quite enough of the military reminiscences. Not in mixed company.' A low, deeply measured voice interrupted, with the over-clipped resonances of the old-school army officer. The sort that Alasdair actively tried to avoid at every opportunity. He began to curse Melissa silently in his head for landing him in this melee for a whole weekend.

'Colonel Gauntlet at your service, ex India, so we three will have much in common, what.' He clapped Alasdair hard on the back, almost making him stumble.

'Ah yes, my father,' Davinia cut in. 'Come on over here, Alasdair and Melissa. There are a couple of spare chairs by this table.' She sounded agitated; had she realised a rescue mission was in order?

Melissa led Alasdair over and put his hand on the back of what appeared to be a solid wooden arts-and-craft-type chair as he could feel the carving on the back. He sat down, reached forward and found the low table. Sheba sat upright on the floor to attention, her nose level with his knee.

'Sherry?' Davinia sounded flustered. 'Mother, come and meet my friends, Melissa and Alasdair.'

The woman who was presented to them as Marjorie Gauntlet, Davinia's mother, was not at all what he had expected for the wife of a military commander. She smelled of roses. Her voice, when she spoke to introduce herself, was soft, delicate and hesitant. She reminded him as he sat down again of a lop-eared rabbit from his childhood. Inquisitive, floppy but instinctively lazy. He couldn't see her running the household here with precision.

'I do hope your room is adequate. I am afraid I leave it all to Davinia and the housekeeper,' she murmured rather vaguely.

'Yes, it is,' Melissa said. 'This is an interesting house, quite out of the way. Is it a family home?'

'Oh yes,' replied Davinia. 'Father inherited it from

an uncle. Gauntlets have been in Somerset for centuries. It suited them to come home from India as Mother's health had been delicate.'

Alasdair wondered, sensing all sorts of undercurrents in this room. He would have to talk to Melissa about it later. Davinia seemed intelligent and open. He sensed a warmth in her that appealed to him. The others he was not at all sure about.

'Let me introduce you both to my brother, Charles, and his wife, Serena. They will be so pleased to have some younger people in the house.'

Melissa squeezed Alasdair's arm and they both automatically stood up to greet them.

'Glad to meet you.' Charles had an Eton drawl and belied his sister's statement by appearing distinctly underwhelmed. Alasdair was used to this; with his disability, people tended to overlook him. Sometimes it was almost as if he was invisible. Charles seemed to perk up when meeting Melissa, though. Alasdair had to resist an outward grimace. The Honourable Melissa Charters, as he well knew, was striking. Her honey-gold bobbed curly hair, her large blue eyes and long legs that suited the shorter-skirted fashion made her a magnet for most men. Clearly Serena thought so too. Her greeting to him had been dripping with sympathy. With Melissa, it had been a clipped, insincere staccato.

Davinia rushed on, sounding a little panicked now. 'And here, let me present you to friends of my parents down for the weekend – Captain Searle and his wife, Elizabeth Searle. They too are home from India.'

Alasdair almost groaned and found he was momentarily devoid of small talk in the face of such military excess.

'How fascinating. I can't wait to hear all about it. I have never been. It sounds an amazing place. You were born there weren't you, Davinia?' Melissa said. She had squeezed his arm and seemed happy to fill in the social chit chat.

'Yes, I was, and Charles too, although he is older than me and was sent home to school before I really got to know him. I was lucky Mother wanted me to stay home with her, so I think I had the best of it. The heat, the colours, the smell of the spices.'

There was the sound of a snort – that could only be Charles poopooing Davinia's thoughts on India, and Alasdair decided he was not sure he liked him any more than the others. The Searles seemed nice enough, and he too hoped to hear all about India. Otherwise it was going to be a long and tedious bore of a weekend.

'Oh, there you are.' Davinia's voice had suddenly gone husky. 'May I present our last guest, Sheridan Kennard, all the way from America.'

'How do, folks? So kind of the Colonel here to invite me. I was tracking down some business while on holiday in these fair isles and here I am.'

Alasdair would dearly have liked to see him. He sounded like the archetypal stage American. Was he wearing a Stetson?

'Haven't you forgotten someone, Davinia?' The voice was high-pitched, thin and belligerent. Quite clearly an elderly lady. Alasdair was reminded of a Pekinese one of his aunts had. Although he could not go so far as to imagine Aunt Petunia would be nipping his ankles.

SIX

FRIDAY DINNER

Melissa watched the flush rise from Davinia's neck to encompass her face. She was not alone in noticing. There was an awkward silence for a moment. But standing there, her face suffused with colour, in her pale blue floaty chiffon dress, not as short as Melissa's but fashionable all the same, Davinia was still beautiful. It was the sort of delicate English rose beauty that could not be marred by any other emotion, except perhaps anger. Was that what it was now?

'Oh Great Aunt Petunia, as if you could be overlooked!' Charles's laconic drawl saved his sister. Melissa was not so sure who it was more to annoy: Davinia or Petunia. There were clearly stormy relationships here. She studied the old woman, dressed head to toe in black, relieved only by the heavy pearls about her neck, her grey hair piled upon her head. A woman who had ensured that she was now the centre of attention, the whole room arrested in movement, their eyes on her. All except Sheridan Kennard – he was still watching Davinia, a look of concern upon his open, square-jawed face; concern and was there admiration? Melissa smiled. She loved matchmaking, and she was very fond of Davinia. She deserved a chance at happiness.

The second gong sounded.

'Wait. Before we go in, I want to sort out about clearing the moat. If it carries on raining tomorrow or the next few days, the banks of the rivers will burst.' The Colonel had puffed his chest out, standing with his legs firmly planted, and was gesturing with his forefinger. He looked like a bellicose rooster.

'And as I said, why me, William? What is wrong with Dunmore? I know he is the chauffeur, but this is something out of the norm. All hands on deck, eh?' Roderick countered.

'Precisely my point in also asking you to help. I'll be there as well. I'm not shirking, man. We have plenty of waders, if you are worried about getting wet!'

Roderick spluttered, and it was his turn to flush. In his case, a rather startling beetroot.

'Listen,' Colonel William continued, his voice lowered but still quite clear to the rest of the party, 'surely I don't need to remind you . . .'

'Roderick, please, the gong has sounded. I cannot be kept waiting at my age. It is late enough. Take me in.' Petunia's high, wavering voice interrupted. Melissa looked at her with interest. This was no wilting old lady; there was steel in her backbone. As if feeling Melissa's eyes on her, she turned her head and stared back at her. Petunia's shrewd dark eyes were still strong, having lost none of the colour in old age. They were the glittering, intelligent eyes of a hawk.

Momentarily taken aback, Melissa shivered and reached down for Alasdair's hand. He took it while rising from the chair in one movement. He was stronger, Melissa realised. Working around on the farm and long walks with Sheba had returned the muscle he had lacked from inactivity. He now was recognisable to her at least as the lithe, fit young man who had married her in some haste on his leave in 1917. She stood there for a moment, lost in her thoughts. Six years and still no sign of—

'What is it?' Alasdair interrupted. 'I am going to need some of your input. There are far too many new people for me to get a handle on thus far.'

'You and me both, buddy,' cut in just one of those people.

Alasdair laughed easily, but it was more to hide his chagrin, Melissa knew. The trouble was, he would have no idea how many of those people were still in the room. 'Now' – Alasdair turned to the source of the voice – 'you are easy, just listen to that accent. I shouldn't think there are many Americans kicking around in Somerset.'

'I suspect not, but I met William Gauntlet up in town, he introduced me to his delightful daughter, Davinia, and I wangled an invite down.'

Davinia flushed prettily. 'Now, now, you naughty man, I know it was really to sort out investments with the family. Sheridan is a consultant.'

'Oh, I am confused. Do you work in a hospital?' Melissa asked.

'No, little lady, I am a financial and management consultant or engineer as it is sometimes called back home.'

'Come on, dears, let us proceed.' Marjorie Gauntlet, clutching a handkerchief to her bejewelled bosom over plum watered silk, with a fluffy stole in pale grey about her shoulders, attempted to shoo them into the hall.

She looks rather like a dithering rabbit. Melissa smiled, guiding Alasdair out of the room and following the tripping gait of Marjorie Gauntlet.

Then a thought struck her. She looked behind her; Davinia and Sheridan were too far away she hoped, so she leant in and whispered in Alasdair's ear. 'Investments, America . . . are you thinking what I am thinking?'

'No doubt. Bernard Lyons.' He spat the words out softly, but his anger was evident. 'He went to America and no doubt is still an investment banker, making money.'

'If he was responsible for Cousin Emma's death, as we think, then Sheridan could be our chance to trace him!'

SEVEN

The dining room was as infinitely gloomy as the rest of the house. There were candelabra with candles on the table, but they had lost their lustre and were tarnished, so they added to the general gloom. The candles, clearly of cheap quality, flickered and waved and looked in danger of guttering before the meal started.

Perhaps, Melissa thought, there was a draught. When she listened, the storm could still be heard: the rain on the window not quite masked by the heavy brocade curtains and the spit of the fire as droplets reached it. She looked at the butler. The low lighting put his features in reflection, shadows trailing across his gaunt face, and she realised that he was quite old, well into his seventies, but whereas at Pennstone the butler appeared sprightly, this man appeared ill. He turned and lit two standard lamps, creating more light in the room. Melissa had not noticed them initially. Why hadn't they put in wall lights? Perhaps they only replaced when they had to. With all these people living here, they could not be short of money. Why else was Sheridan here but to chase the money opportunities and perhaps have a dalliance with Davinia? No, she hoped it wasn't a dalliance but that he was serious. Davinia did deserve that chance at happiness.

They were seated down towards the end of the table. Marjorie, as was traditional, was seated at the end opposite, with her husband at the head. He still seemed to be bickering loudly with his cousin Roderick. Either side of Marjorie were the Searles. Clearly they were old friends, and they were ensconced in a bubble of their shared friendship and memories, not in challenging or entertaining any other guests. They had been briefly introduced in the drawing room, and it appeared that they were not so interested in acquainting themselves further with Melissa and Alasdair now. Melissa was seated next to Captain – had she heard his Christian name? – Searle. And across the table from Elizabeth Searle.

Next to Melissa, thankfully, was Alasdair. She glanced at the settings and signalled to the butler; his name remained a mystery still. She asked him to replace Alasdair's long-stemmed glasses for flat-bottomed water glasses. He raised his eyebrows but the replacement was done. She looked across the table and caught a look of utter scorn from Charles, who was sitting opposite her, but then it flitted away and he inclined his head to her in acknowledgement with a bland smile. Melissa smiled sweetly but insincerely back. In that moment, she realised that this weekend was going to be an uphill struggle. That in her desire to please Davinia, as far as Alasdair was concerned she may have made a terrible mistake. These were no family and friends willing Alasdair to succeed but strangers with inbuilt prejudices against the permanently war wounded.

With the glasses replaced, she relaxed. Alasdair found long-stemmed glasses hard to cope with, being too easy to knock over. After six years of marriage, and five of them with his blindness, she was learning what helped him. Melissa leant in towards him. 'So, we have Marjorie to our left at the foot and William at the head. To his right, we have Sheridan, Davinia, Serena opposite you, Charles across from me, then Elizabeth Searle. Our side from Marjorie, on my left is Captain Searle, then me, you, Petunia and Roderick.'

'So, Sheridan Kennard is guest of honour. Interesting. Strictly speaking, as an Honourable it should be you,' he whispered back.

'Oh, you know I don't care about that sort of thing.'

'Yes, but it shows a certain mentality.' Alasdair tapped her thigh under the table. 'An innate prejudice or superior carelessness. Could be indicative of more than a seating plan, don't you know? Watch and learn.'

EIGHT

Alasdair stopped abruptly as a sharp elbow dug into his ribs from his right-hand side.

'What are you two blathering about?' the sharp voice of Petunia cut in.

Melissa tensed up beside him, no doubt readying a retort, but Alasdair, a hand on her thigh under the table, beat her to it. 'My wife was just apprising me of the table arrangements so I know where everyone is.' He turned his head and smiled at her.

There was a quick intake of breath and then Petunia cackled. 'Clever, aren't you? I could almost think you can see me.' There was a movement and a rush of air. Alasdair did not flinch. He was getting used to this now that he got about more: people suspecting he was bluffing about his blindness and waving their hands in front of his eyes.

'Good gad, Mother, do you have to wave your arms around? Anyone would think you were a true harridan.' Roderick guffawed loudly at his attempt at a joke, but it cut off with a grunt. Alasdair suspected Petunia's right bony elbow was stronger than her left, and that had hurt.

'Honestly, Great Aunt, a bit of decorum would be welcomed occasionally.' It was the high-pitched slow drawl of a studied aristocrat. Serena, Alasdair surmised. What was her background? His deliberations were interrupted by the arrival of the first course: soup,

Brown Windsor, he would recognise the smell anywhere. He just hoped it was good and not full of gristle.

But Petunia hadn't finished. 'Don't airs and grace me, Serena, dear. You weren't so upper crust as to be invited to the wedding, were you. Bet you went, didn't you?' Another sharp jab in the ribs ensued for Alasdair.

Alasdair, not wanting to be drawn into this, mumbled into his soup.

'Oh, darling, she means Bertie and Elizabeth's wedding in April. Yes, we were there. There was an awful crush in the Abbey. Of course, we are not quite in those circles, but my grandfather and father were there in their ermine.' Alasdair could tell Melissa had tried to make it light and faintly deprecating, but he rather felt she might not have made too many friends around the table all the same.

'Gosh, how exciting.' Davinia's exquisite husky voice floated across the expanse. 'We must catch up and you can tell me all about it. I want to know all about the fashions. Melissa is the granddaughter of His Grace Baron Clifford, you know.'

Petunia cackled again. 'Ha, a real aristocrat, not a wishful one.' Spite crackled in the air.

Too late, Melissa must have realised the trap she had been led into by the wicked old woman. 'Well, um, not really, we are very low on the pecking order.'

'And Alasdair, your father is Sir Hector Charters, isn't he, barrister to royalty? I bet you could keep us entertained with his cases.' Davinia, strangely, seemed happy to side with Petunia against her sister-in-law. Alasdair was surprised as it seemed so out of character.

'Gee, but wouldn't they have to lock you up in the

Tower for divulging family secrets?' The attempt on being disingenuous from Sheridan worked. It interrupted the baiting and the table laughed politely. A small silence ensued as they finished their soup.

It actually wasn't bad, Alasdair reflected. He had, he thought, actually found a couple of pieces of beef in it.

The next course was, of course, fish. It was some sort of fillet in a parsley sauce. Alasdair could tell it was fish from its consistency and, worryingly, the smell, but he could not say what it was. Mercifully, it was a very small portion. He worried about this adherence to Edwardian-style dinners in the country, especially for these weekend parties, as they now seemed to be called. Were the people around him inordinately fat? He knew he would be if he repeated this every weekend.

The jibe, when it came, took him by surprise, but perhaps he was fair game after Melissa had been set up.

'Tell me, Charters, how was your war?'

NINE

Melissa stared at Charles; she was sure her mouth had dropped open. She realised that Petunia, no flies on her, had set Melissa up earlier, thus putting his wife, Serena, in a poor light. Was this Charles's way of getting revenge? But how? Alasdair was a war hero. Did he not realise that? Or was he banking on Alasdair's innate British understatement to make a point?

'It went,' Alasdair replied laconically. As Melissa had predicted, he was clearly not going to be drawn into any such discussion, and he could not mention his work in the Secret Intelligence Service.

'But you got the DSO and bar and the rank of major, hardly to be sniffed at!' Davinia said firmly. 'Don't be such a pill, Charles. It isn't as if you did an awful lot, is it?'

'Humph, he was in a protected profession running this estate for most of it,' his father, Colonel William, stated, looking embarrassed. 'It was only when I was called up to the tribunals that we felt he should go in on active service to set an example, what?' The look he shot his daughter would have reduced the other ranks to a quivering wreck.

Davinia just smiled sweetly back. Melissa, remembering the war wounded they had visited and Davinia's dead fiancé, suddenly realised that this family seethed with resentment. What had she got herself and

Alasdair into?

'The tribunals? Sorry, as an American I am a bit lost here.' He sounded genuine enough to Melissa, but there was a sparkle in his eyes that belied it. She just knew he was up to some mischief.

'Local appeal tribunals, checking people's credentials, don't you know,' Colonel William blustered. He looked extremely uncomfortable; his face had paled and he was not making eye contact.

Melissa shifted her attention to Charles. He was red in the face and there was fear in his eyes. She glanced down at Roderick and his face was streaked with venom. She could now see the family resemblance with Petunia. Like mother, like son.

'I presume, Alasdair, that you spent some actual time in the trenches?' Roderick queried.

'Yes, I was there for nearly two years. Then I was assigned to another role due to my languages.' His voice was casual, but Melissa felt his knee jigging under the table.

'A cushy job, with the staff, I suppose,' Charles muttered.

'No, dear, that was you, and in London,' Davinia muttered poisonously, not quite low enough that it could not be heard around most of the table.

Roderick gave a sharp guffaw, throwing his head back; he had a rather over-long, full head of white hair swept back from the forehead. Thinking of Africa, Melissa pictured those black-and-white photographs she had seen of hyenas. What did they sound like? Like that?

'Hah,' Roderick said. 'Now I know one when I see

one. Way off the mark, Charles old bean. This one was tricksie. Hush, hush and covert ops. He won't admit it, he can't, but I bet you he was a spy.'

Luckily, Alasdair was saved from answering by the next course arriving. Veal al la Viennoise, Melissa thought, or at least some thinly sliced meat in breadcrumbs. She grimaced; usually it was hard and tough but, delight of delights, this was cooked well, succulent and tasty.

'That was a bit near the knuckles,' she muttered in Alasdair's ear.

'Yes, but revealing. I had it quite wrong – they don't like each other much this family, do they?'

Melissa looked up, nervous that they might be overheard. Not seeing people's faces, Alasdair often missed the nuances of their expressions: boredom, a desire to interrupt or someone taking too much interest. She glanced down the table. Charles opposite was scowling into his food. His wife looked like she had picked up a bad smell and was trying not to acknowledge it. Davinia was smiling into her plate. But Sheridan, at the end next to their host, was clearly half listening to an interminable story – about India, it sounded. At the same time, his sharp eyes were missing nothing. He caught her looking at him and his face and eyes once again became bland. This was a man worth watching, she thought. What he was up to? However, he was a newcomer to the household, so surely he could not have anything to do with the death of Davinia's grandmother.

TEN

The wall lights began to flicker rather ominously. Melissa automatically stiffened. Alasdair rested his hand on her knee and whispered, 'What is it?'

'Nothing, I am being silly. Just the lights flickering,' she whispered back.

'William, oh William,' Marjorie called out delicately. 'The lights.'

'Don't worry, old girl, just a battery switching over. I keep telling you.'

'But what if they fail?'

'No reason to fail. Don't worry.'

Marjorie sighed and resumed a conversation with Elizabeth Searle once more, which seemed to consist solely of her anxiety and health issues, as far as Melissa could hear.

Melissa shifted her attention to the far end of the table where William was once again grumbling to his cousin – in a lower voice now, hoping perhaps his wife would not hear him.

'This is why we need to clear the damn moat, you and Charles. The dynamo and the boilers are in the cellars. If we don't clear it, they may flood, and then there will be hell to pay.'

'Oh, Father, don't be so dramatic. They have never flooded,' Charles drawled.

'Not in your lifetime, no, but the villagers are saying

this could be the big one.'

'That is just a way of them trying to get extra work. They think because we are so isolated they have us over a barrel.'

'Well actually, they do. We are isolated, and getting help of any kind it is extremely hard, as you should know. This will one day be yours, and you should be taking more of an interest. We were da— jolly lucky to get Miss Richards for your children.'

'Miss Richards?' Melissa asked.

'The nanny and governess for our children. She often joins us for meals, but tonight we would have been thirteen.' Serena Gauntlet had perfected a way of looking down her nose like a camel and at the same time effecting quite a passable aristocratic drawl but not quite managing it. There was an unmistakable burr in there somewhere. Not that Melissa herself was snobbish. But putting on an accent just tended to make things worse, and she rather liked the West Country accent.

'Oh yes, Serena, dear,' Marjorie managed. 'Quite too, too worrying. I can be very superstitious, you know.' She made it sound like a serious affliction.

Melissa wondered where the poor governess was being forced to eat her meal. Probably in the nursery.

'Yes, it is really rather an interesting story,' Serena continued. 'She appeared here out of the blue with excellent references asking if there was a job just when we were thinking we needed someone. I can cope with one small child, but two?' She rolled her eyes and shivered dramatically.

Good grief, thought Melissa, we are in a house full of Sarah Bernhardts – or worse, a second-rate farce.

'I mean, Grandma used to help a bit, but it was not really a suitable arrangement. So, you can see she appeared like a gift from heaven.'

'I presume her references were valid?' Melissa commented drily; her idea of gifts from heaven was rather more cynical.

'Oh, I hope I am a good enough judge of character,' Serena replied haughtily, but, as if answering a snort from Aunt Petunia, added, 'And she has been absolutely wonderful since we engaged her. All of, what was it – six months ago? Were you here then, Uncle Roderick?'

'What, what?' Roderick had the glassy-eyed and flushed-cheek demeanour of the heavy drinker. Melissa had noticed that he had been drinking steadily throughout the meal so far.

'Oh wake up, boy,' Petunia trilled. 'They are checking your bona fides now.'

She turned her sulphurous gaze on Serena and then down the table to Melissa. 'Yes, my son was here then. He had returned directly from South Africa and is still here, resplendent in the bosom of his family.'

Serena coloured under Petunia's gaze. Did she resent all these relations living here? It certainly could not be cheap. It might be useful to find out the financial arrangements. Who paid for what? How long were they staying? Were they guests or lodgers? Quite clearly, it was not all sweetness and light. Enough to result in murder?

ELEVEN

Alasdair had let the conversation swirl around him. He listened but less for the content and more for the nuances behind the speech. They were much more revealing. At the current moment, he was concerned about Melissa. She was seriously rattled and that was unusual. He had been impressed with her handling of the murders at Pennstone Manor last year. She had then thrown herself into the renovation and changes to the house itself so that they could live alongside her aunt and uncle but separately. The work was all but finished. Was she now bored? Is that why they had come on this wild goose chase?

True, the work he himself had been supervising on the estate was now, in the winter, at a lull. The Brigadier could deal with any emergencies that cropped up, and Davies, the estate manager, was more than competent. Alasdair smiled. He realised all of a sudden, surprised, that for the first time since he had been blinded in the war he felt almost contentment. The demons were still there, lurking, but for the moment they were in abeyance.

Why were they here then? Was Melissa restless once more? Surely Pennstone was enough of a challenge for her talents. Why had she answered the call from Davinia? What did she feel she owed her? He knew they had corresponded since the war, but if they were such great friends why had she not come to stay? Had he been so difficult that she felt she could not ask him? That she felt she ought to ask for permission and was doubtful of the answer? His mood changed and grew darker, the barbs and tension around the table seeming to reflect his own feelings. The dark shadows in the ill-lit room seemed almost tangible to his senses.

This was a family that did not enjoy living together. Had it always been thus or had the death of Davinia's grandmother tipped the balance? How on earth did she expect them to investigate something that looked so innocuous? Old people died; many had died during the flu epidemic in 1919. Every winter it seemed that the populace held their breath in case another strain returned, but though people got flu, on the whole, unless they were already weakened by old age, illness or poverty, they did not die. Blimey, he was beginning to sound like Melissa, but the political situation worried him. He was long overdue a meeting with his father; he always had a finger on the pulse of the seat of power as a barrister to the aristocracy, many of whom were elected members of the government. He ought to know what was going on.

He tuned in to the argument between William and Roderick. Argument? No, perhaps bickering was more correct. He could understand William's concerns. He hoped he would take him around the estate. He was interested in the fact that here they had put everything in the cellars. Was that below the servants' halls and kitchens? At Pennstone, the boilers were under the house – easier for the coal to be delivered down a chute. But the generators, new from Lister–Bruston, ran on petrol, and the tank and equipment were now housed in their own separate area made from the inside of the barn across the courtyard. Safe they may have assured him it was, but the thought of bringing petrol into their home had worried him. He assumed the comments about the lights meant here they were on an older system with storage batteries. He hoped someone was maintaining them. Melissa had said that the house was 'positively gothic,' but he rather thought that having to use candles and oil lamps would be going too far for the sighted.

The pudding was removed, but Alasdair could not have said what it was: something creamy, spongey, with fruit. The fruit gave off no smell so he assumed from the cloying sweetness that they were tinned, hardly surprising in winter.

Now he supposed he would have to sit here while the women left and the men smoked cigars and drivelled over large amounts of port. He flipped his Braille watch open, he hoped surreptitiously, under the tablecloth. Nearly eleven o'clock. He yawned. He was dog tired; it had been a long day. Coping with the sighted world was exhausting, as was the strain of maintaining his sangfroid. However, keeping up the mask was draining but essential. He would not let the darkness in. Not again. Sheba shifted under his chair as if sensing his mood change. He stroked her head to reassure her.

***

Melissa noticed the yawn. How soon could they reasonably be expected to bunk off to bed? They hadn't seen the rest of the house yet, and she wanted them up and early to get the advantage before most of the household and guests were about. The windows rattled and the lights dimmed again. She hoped this damn storm and rain would abate as even when they finally got to bed, it was going to be a noisy night. She yawned herself, hastily suppressed but not before she saw that Davinia had noticed. She seemed to smile in sympathy and then dipped her head as if in acknowledgement.

'Alasdair and Melissa, you must be exhausted. It is such a long haul down here, even from the New Forest. Daddy, do you mind if we leave you and I will show them what's what?'

With a flick of his wrist and a wave, they were dismissed, and Melissa, extracting Alasdair neatly from the table, tucked his hand under her elbow and they left the room. Sheba, on her lead, padded in front of them.

Davinia led them towards a drawing room. 'Would you like coffee and liqueurs? I can have cheese and biscuits sent up to you if you wish?'

'Actually, you know, Davinia, could we just have some cocoa?' Melissa stifled another yawn. 'Would it be frightfully rude if we turned in? I want to be fresh for tomorrow.'

'Yes, so do I,' Alasdair said. 'Will you come and find us? Now we have met I presume everyone bar the governess, then we should be able to make more sense of what you are after. I assume that you exempt the staff?'

'Gosh, on the trail already. I am impressed. I will go through the staff with you. Much as I would prefer it was one of them involved, I think it is unlikely. No, you heard them tonight – it is far more likely, as you said, that it is one of us.' She raised a hand to stall the remark she saw forming on Alasdair's face and then realised it was wasted. 'No, no, Alasdair, don't say it. I know it may all be hogwash.'

'Hogwash?' Melissa giggled. 'How long have you spent with the yank? He seems to be rubbing off on you.'

Davinia coloured prettily. 'He has only been here a few days but he is rather nice, isn't he? A breath of fresh air. I do hope you will like him too.'

'What is there not to like?' Alasdair was clearly getting grumpy. He wanted his sleep, and Melissa suspected he considered it was not the time for girl talk.

'Tomorrow, Davinia, catch us then and we can have a long chat, but I really think we must go to bed.'

'Wait, I will just give you an oil lamp to take up, just in case the lights fail. They don't usually, but Daddy is jumpy about this storm. Not surprising, really. It has been going on for days. We are all feeling a little ropey. It gets on one's nerves, you know.'

Perhaps, thought Melissa, accepting the lamp and a box of matches, that might explain the tension at dinner, but somehow she had an uncomfortable feeling that there was more to it. Much more.

TWELVE

'Wait, Sheba, she needs to be let out.' Alasdair squeezed Melissa's arm.

'Oh gosh. Shall I do it? Or fetch Thomas?' Melissa wanted to avoid the storm.

'No, I must be there at all times – that is the advice from both Lieutenant-Colonel Richardson and the school in Oldenburg.'

They slipped out of the front door and were afforded scant protection from the elements in the porch as Sheba dashed not very far and returned quickly.

'Rather galling that the Germans got there first,' she mused, rubbing her arms furiously.

'Yes, Blindführhund. Guide dog sounds much better, don't you think? Can you imagine the reaction here if I dropped that word in conversation?'

'Come on in. It is freezing.' She pushed open the front door and pulled him inside, not quick enough as Sheba rushed in and shook herself.

'Yuck, let's go before they notice the mess.' She giggled. 'You know, I am beginning to think that anything we might say here could have repercussions. Still, they have been very indulgent of Sheba. So far.'

'Enough. Let's go to the privacy of our room.' He reached down and attached Sheba's lead.

'Have you thought any more about using a harness like in Oldenburg?'

'No.'

His clipped reply told her the conversation was at an end; he was still prickly about attempts by her to breach the shell of his blindness. She gave up, took his arm and led the way up the stairs to their room. Once in the room, she collapsed into a chair and watched Alasdair take the lead off Sheba. She ran to a folded blanket in the corner and lay down. Alasdair, his face creased with concentration, made his way unerringly to the bed. He sat on the edge. Only the deep sigh as he relaxed revealed the amount of effort and tension held in his body to achieve his goal.

Melissa pulled off her shoes and began to undress. She crossed to the bed and felt under her pillow for her pyjama case. She blessed the new fashion for pyjamas and had a lovely pair in peach silk. They hadn't felt very warm for cold winter houses, but luckily Alasdair was like a furnace. She also had a pair of matching silk socks in case her feet were cold.

Alasdair was still sitting slumped on the end of the bed. She changed quickly, took off her make-up with Nivea and went and brushed her teeth. He was still sitting there. His pyjamas were all laid out still. She pushed aside the blankets and eiderdown and slipped into bed. It was this movement that seemed to rouse him.

He grabbed his pyjamas and went to the bathroom. When he came out, his clothes were neatly folded. He walked across the room and laid them on a chair. Melissa was impressed but knew better than to comment. Firstly, he would probably resent it, and secondly, he would be counting his steps.

He whisked back the covers and launched himself into the bed. Pulling up the covers, he reached for Melissa. 'Let's forget about them, the storm and the cold. I have an excellent idea about generating heat.'

THIRTEEN

The next morning, they were up early. Certainly they were the only people appearing at that time for breakfast. Replete after a good full English – bacon, sausage, fried eggs, fried bread, mushrooms and tomatoes – they decided to brave the weather and take Sheba for a quick walk before meeting with Davinia. A short walk down the drive, they came to a low bridge that must have been obscured by the rain and the dark last night. It seemed to be to cross the 'moat' or stream that surrounded the house. Near the bridge, someone was toiling waist-high in the water. Water that seemed to be gaining height even as Melissa watched.

'Gosh, that looks dangerous. The water is definitely rising. Alasdair, there is someone working in it. 'Everything all right?' she called. The man with grey hair had his back to her and raised his arm in acknowledgement but did not turn and continued slashing at the vegetation with a vicious-looking billhook, seemingly oblivious to the water swirling about him. 'Gosh, he looks far too occupied. I have no idea who it is but he is all alone. What happened to the others?'

'Come on, let's explore further.' Alasdair felt the need after the large breakfast to stride out, and the fresh air, even though it was drizzling quite heavily now, was at least refreshing. Thank goodness for their investment in Warm coats.

They walked a little further down the drive, but Melissa was deterred by the large puddles. 'I should have borrowed some gumboots, and you will need them too if we are to go further. The drive is now blocked by huge puddles.'

Alasdair turned his head from side to side. 'Extraordinary smell, this place has. Quite different from the New Forest. How would you describe it? Peaty, boggy? Phew, quite a wind as well, I suppose it is because we are on a hill and the rest is flat?'

'To be honest, they have quite a lot of trees and shrubs about the place and I cannot see from here. Let's go around the house and see what there is and I can try and describe it to you.'

Despite walking for a good fifteen minutes, Melissa still could see nothing of the countryside. It was most strange to her. Why live on a hill if you didn't want views? She said as much to Alasdair.

'Perhaps they need the cover to protect from the wind?' he muttered, pulling his muffler closer to his neck and tucking the stray ends firmly into his coat.

They rounded the far side of the house and were approaching where they had started. The labourer appeared to have given up as she couldn't see him. Thinking it rather odd, she moved them closer. Then she gave a gasp. 'Oh my goodness, there has been an accident. He is floating face down in the water amongst the reeds!'

She made to rush forward but Alasdair held her. 'Stop, don't you go in after him. Leave me and go up to the house for help.'

Melissa pelted up the drive yelling, 'Help, help!'

No one appeared. She flung open the front door and stood in the hall and bellowed between gasps of breath, recovering from the running.

The butler appeared first. 'Call a doctor,' she ordered. 'There has been an accident.'

Then Serena appeared. 'Delay that order.' The butler paused mid-stride. 'What on earth do you think you are doing?' she exclaimed, with a look a classically prepared prefect might pose when faced with a third former running in the corridor – a case of outraged indignation par excellence.

Exasperated – mercifully she had never been to school and did not recognise the pose, just the high dudgeon – Melissa shouted back full throttle, 'There is someone floating face down in your moat and I don't think they are swimming!'

'What?' Charles had appeared, 'Serena, find Father. Ring for the doctor, you fool.'

The butler continued his stride towards the phone cubicle under the stairs.

'Come on, show me,' Charles instructed Melissa. There was slightly less Eton to the drawl.

'It is by the bridge,' she yelled as he set off at quite a pace with her struggling to keep up. Sheba let off a volley of barking as they arrived at the spot Melissa had left her and Alasdair. Running a little behind Charles, she saw him jump into the moat and turn the body over.

FOURTEEN

Recalling it later, Alasdair was hard pressed to accurately place the emotion in Charles's voice as he realised who the body was. A huge splash then lots of water swooshing and then a gasp. Silence and, finally, a cry of 'Father, Father!' It was shock, surprise, certainly, and something between horror and anguish, but was there also an inkling of relief?

Melissa clutched Alasdair's arm, her breath heaving. 'They are calling for a doctor. Oh, Roderick, has the butler got through?' she called.

Alasdair's shoulders drooped in frustration and impotence having to stand there like a lemon wondering what on earth was happening.

'No idea,' Roderick replied. 'Heard the shouting and have followed on.' He paused, then, 'Oh hell, Charles.'

'Come on, Uncle, help me get him in.'

'Roderick has also jumped in,' Melissa explained. 'Anyone know artificial respiration?'

'Bloody waste of time that,' Roderick commented. 'He has got a ruddy great divot in the back of his head. Shut that dog up.'

Alasdair, reminding himself that everyone reacted differently under stress and that Roderick Gauntlet ought, by rights, to have a huge hangover this morning, said nothing and bent and soothed her. Sheba quietened.

Melissa exclaimed, 'There is a long-handled rake on

the bank, oh, and a fork. Any sign of the billhook?' she called. 'And here is the butler. Can you help them get him out?'

She watched, explaining what was happening for Alasdair as Roderick clambered out and, with the butler, hauled William Gauntlet onto the bank. Then he pulled out Charles.

'I am not sure we should have moved the body,' Alasdair said. 'The police will need to be informed.'

'Have some respect. This is my father you are talking about,' Charles snapped, 'And what do you mean about the police?'

'I doubt he hit himself on the back of the head. Don't touch the implements,' Alasdair shouted just as he heard someone pick up the tools lying on the bank.

'Oh, Roderick.' Melissa sighed. 'You will have messed up any fingerprints now.'

'Fingerprints? Fingerprints? What are you two morons wittering about?'

'They are suggesting, quite rightly, that Father may very well have been murdered.' Alasdair jumped as Davinia spoke in a trembling low voice while resting her hand on his free arm, and he thought she was soothing Sheba who, although was sitting to heel, was clearly agitated from her twitching movements.

'Best not to pet her,' Alasdair said firmly. 'It distracts her while she is working.' He turned and smiled at Davinia, who was clearly distressed and needed soothing herself, to take the edge off the rebuke.

'Quite all right, Alasdair. I too am distracted and upset. I am sorry. Dr Haymes is away on a case, near the western border. He is the only doctor for fifty miles.

They are sending the district nurse.'

'Then we must contact the police. They may have a police surgeon.'

'In the middle of the Levels?' Charles exploded. 'The nearest centre is Taunton.'

'Thomas has brought a blanket to cover up Colonel Gauntlet. Oh and spares for those who are wet.' Melissa's voice was cool.

'Hot bath is what's required now,' said Roderick, 'and a stiff drink. Come on, m'boy.'

Alasdair was frankly bemused. Colonel Gauntlet was lying on the bank dead and they were going off for baths and whisky. What sort of family was this?

'Wait for me,' called Davinia. 'I will contact the police.'

'Anything I can do, sir?' Thomas asked of Alasdair.

'Well, this is going to get tricky. What has happened to the chauffeur? Doesn't he double as a handyman too?'

'He wasn't at breakfast apparently, and that is unusual.'

There was suddenly a strange whooshing noise and a gurgling. 'What the hell is that?' Alasdair said.

'Good heavens, darling, it's the water! It is rising – and quickly. We have to move the body!' Melissa exclaimed.

'Thomas, could you lift him? No, far too heavy. Right, then. Lead me to his feet. You take the shoulders, Thomas, and navigate the way backwards. Melissa, you steer us and take Sheba. And bring the gardening tools.'

It was a weary little procession that made its way to the house. The water was steadily rising behind them. Just as they got there, someone swished past on a bicycle, throwing up an avalanche of water.

'Sorry,' cried a female voice, 'I was one wheel ahead of the water all the way. Luckily I was just down the village. I think we're marooned here. Blimey, is that the patient? I think I can declare life extinct from here!'

'I say, we are guests here. Yes, he is dead. Where shall we put him?' Melissa asked, straining with her guiding and handling an agitated dog.

'No telling when the waters'll recede. Look, bring him into the hall, you look pooped. Pop him down and then we can regroup.' There was the sound of a bicycle being tipped against a wall. Alasdair, Thomas and Melissa carried on into the hall and deposited the body on the floor.

'Hello, I'm Rosalind Foote, the district nurse.'

There was then a silence.

'Oh sorry, Nurse Foote, my husband is blind. Alasdair, hold out your hand, she wants to shake it.'

It was shaken vigorously.

'Well, well. Gas? Shell? Natural causes?'

Alasdair was not used to such plain speaking but rather liked it. He smiled. 'Blow to the back of the head, detached retinas.'

'Interesting. I sense a story.' There was the sound of hands rubbing, 'Still, we'll have plenty of time to delve into medical histories. I'd better let them know they're likely to have another guest. I'm told last time they had flooding like this it took a week to subside. Still, I can think of worse places to be cooped up in.'

'Not with a resident murderer,' muttered Alasdair.

FIFTEEN

'If you're guests, then I will have to find the rest of the family. Excepting the one at our feet. Excuse me. Oi, anyone about? Nurse Foote here,' she bellowed. There was a slight trace of a northern accent. 'So, who're you?'

'Thomas. Valet to Mr Charters here.'

'Bet you were his batman, weren't you?' She shoved his shoulder.

'Yes, but . . .'

'Amazing the number of you who stayed together in civvy street. But – significantly – not in this house, despite the military careers. Perhaps that explains this. Thomas, help me turn him over. Bring the rake.'

'Well, he certainly took a bash on the back of the head,' Melissa said.

Nurse Foote held the back edge of the rake head over the wound. 'Looks like a match, I'd say. Of course, it'll need a doctor to confirm it.' She knelt over him, turned his head and began pumping his ribs. Water trickled out from his mouth onto the polished floor.

'Yuck. What are you doing?' Melissa exclaimed.

'Won't save him now but proves water in the lungs. He drowned. So bashed on the head, enough to render him unconscious? Very well. Thomas, lend me a hand. Undo his shirt and take off the tie. Really, dressing up like this to clear a ditch?'

'You are going to undress him here?' Melissa

sounded appalled.

'I need witnesses and you aren't, I presume, related to him or anyone present in the house?'

'No, thank God,' Alasdair muttered.

'OK, now, just pull down the back of his jacket and shirt. I want to see his upper back. There! See it? Come and look, Thomas, and you, young woman. Bruising. Same width as the rake head, do you think? Near as damn it. So I'd say . . .'

'Hit on the head to daze him or knock him out and then held underwater by the same rake until he drowned,' Alasdair completed.

'Yes, well surmised. But knocked out, I think. Come on, quick, Thomas, get him properly dressed, quick, quick before someone comes.' The nurse was all efficiency.

He was dressed, turned over onto his back and re-covered with a blanket just in time for Marjorie and Davinia to appear, closely followed by Serena.

Marjorie began wailing. 'Who is it? Not William. Not William. Please?'

Davinia rushed forward and twitched back the blanket. 'Oh, Daddy.' At which point Marjorie fainted, hitting her head on the floor. Serena started screaming hysterically, and Davinia, turning a neat 360 degrees on her back foot, slapped her, before going to kneel beside her prostrate mother.

Nurse Foote went out of the front door and came back in with her bag. She handed Davinia a small bottle. 'Smelling salts. Come on now, Mrs Gauntlet.' Marjorie remained unresponsive. Nurse Foote then raised her head onto her lap. 'Nasty bump. Always the way, never think to faint on the carpet, has to be the hardwood floor. Typical. Living before the dead, then. We need to get her upstairs to bed. Where're all the other men?'

'Major Roderick Gauntlet and Charles Gauntlet got the body out so were soaked through. There was talk of baths. The butler was soaked to the knees so presumably is drying off somewhere. The chauffeur handyman has gone missing. Davinia, do you have footmen or valets left in the house?' Melissa asked.

'No. We will have to manage by ourselves until the brave men come back.' Davinia's tone was scathing.

'We could put her on a sofa?' suggested Melissa.

'But then we'd have to move her again. We will have to manage.' Nurse Foote appeared to size up the collected souls. 'Fine. Thomas, you take her under the armpits. You, girl, help him at that end. Davinia, you take one leg and you, Serena. Sorry, Mrs Gauntlet, forgetting myself, too familiar.' She winked at Melissa. 'Take the other. I'll take the middle and supervise, and for heaven's sake do not drop her.'

'But it is two flights,' Serena protested.

'And she is your mother-in-law and in need of help. Chop chop. Oh and you, the blind one. Stay here and watch the body.' If she noticed the obvious paradox in her order, she failed to acknowledge it.

SIXTEEN

Alasdair stood where he was, Sheba hunkered down beside him, and he waited, and waited. He listened. There was not a sound, other than the normal creaking to be expected with such an old house. A house that even smelled old, musty, of antique wood and damp. The wind outside had picked up again and he fancied he could hear rain. He became aware that his feet were wet and he was cold.

There was an underlying smell of stagnant water too that seemed to emanate from the corpse somewhere in front of him. He took a few steps back. What if the poor chap was now lying in a pool of water?

Who had killed him? And why? Or perhaps, he thought, the question should be why now? Had Melissa and his visit set this chain of events off? He wished someone would come, even if it was that bastard Charles. Used to being in close proximity to people – Melissa and Thomas in their small service flat in London for years, and now living in Pennstone Manor with the Brigadier and Honor, plus their generous retinue of domestic staff – he was thrown by being left to his own devices. For years in the service he had worked alone and been happy. He had claimed he wanted to be alone for years, but now he realised it quite unnerved him. Was his change of heart due to the fact that last time he had genuinely been on his own, he had lost his sight?

He gave a wry smile. Yes, that could put you off being alone too often.

He grimaced again, thinking of the domestic staff. He noticed that he had automatically used Melissa's preferred wording. She had banned the use of the word 'servants' at Pennstone. They were called staff. He smiled. He did love her, even if he did not express it often, probably not enough, but then he was British. And in loving her, he let her lead them into situations like this. Alasdair, all alone and palely loitering. He shifted his balance; his feet really were wet, his wool socks soggy. Damn and bloody blast, where was everyone in this mausoleum? This waiting around was getting on his nerves.

As if in answer, he heard a door shut and ponderous heavy steps approaching. The butler?

'Sir, what is happening? Sorry I have been so long. I needed to change into dry clothes.'

Glad he was correct and it was the butler, he answered, 'At the sight of her husband, Mrs Gauntlet – Mrs William Gauntlet, I should say – has fainted and knocked herself out. Nurse Foote is in charge. They are all carrying her upstairs up into her room. Tell me, where are the rest of the domestic staff?'

A door opened further down the hall.

'Sir, what are you doing in the Colonel's study?' The butler sounded aghast.

'Oh, I was looking for a private telephone and then got distracted. I decided to make some notes.' Sheridan Kennard was trying to sound sheepish but Alasdair thought he was not quite making it convincing enough to his own acute hearing. There was something odd about him. More than being an American. Alasdair turned towards him. There was a sharp intake of breath.

'Do you know, that wacky dame last night was not so far off. You are one cool dude. I could swear you can see me.'

'Well, I can assure you I cannot. However, I can hear you. Your accent is interesting . . . but you are right, we need the telephone. We must call the police. Nurse Foote has confirmed that in her opinion on checking the body, Colonel Gauntlet was murdered.'

Sheridan whistled. 'Colonel Gauntlet, you say, not the Major?' He sounded shocked. There were hurried footsteps. Alasdair assumed Sheridan was checking the body, and then he whistled again. 'Say, you are right. This is the Colonel. No offence, but who would want to do the old boy in?'

'And why do you think someone might want to do the Major in?' Alasdair countered.

'Sirs, I regret to inform you, but the telephone is dead.'

SEVENTEEN

'Dead?' Sheridan spluttered. 'Whaddaya mean dead?'

'The phone appears, sir, not to be working,' the butler intoned.

'For goodness sake, go and check, Sheridan, this is serious,' Alasdair ordered. This really wasn't the time for polite chitchat, and in his opinion, someone needed to take charge of this bizarre household.

He could hear some rattling and banging. Then Sheridan called, 'Dead as a dodo. I guess the water has got it.'

'Yes, and it is still rising. Can one of you check? Last I heard it was advancing up the drive.'

Someone exited the hall and out the front door in a hurry.

'The water is now at the level of the moat. Just water as far as I can see. What happens now?' Sheridan returned.

'We will be fine up here at the house, the master assured us, but what should we do next, sirs?' The butler was getting rattled; Alasdair could tell from his quavering voice. How old was he? Did butlers go on until they dropped?

'We need to move the body,' Alasdair said firmly. 'What about outbuildings? Have you some that will also not flood? We need to keep it as cold as possible for when the police can arrive.'

'Hey, good call, you sound like a pro. I guess that is why Davinia respects you.' Sheridan sounded thoughtful.

'There is the old potting shed. It is used for storage now but there is not much in it this time of year.'

'How far is it? Alasdair asked; much as he would like dry feet, he knew they had to remove the body out of the sight of the family. 'Look, if I take the feet, can you, Sheridan, manage his shoulders and you . . . I am sorry, what is your name?'

'Dobson, sir.'

'All right, Dobson, you steer us.'

Colonel Gauntlet might have been old but he was quite a weight, and Sheridan and Alasdair were both breathing heavily by the time they had laid out the body on a rather convenient old table in the storehouse. Then Alasdair suddenly realised that having left Sheba sitting in the hall, he would need help getting back. Something must have shown on his face.

'It's OK, buddy, grab my arm and I'll lead you back to the hall. Seen it before, I'll keep you safe. I wouldn't want the responsibility of returning you to that wife of yours damaged, she looks kinda dangerous.'

'Too true.' Alasdair laughed, and then realised he had no qualms about this man on that score at least.

They walked back through the house – the same route as they had left, as far as Alasdair could tell. He would need Melissa to make tactile maps for him. Sheba was pretty good at leading him about now, but she could not tell him where they were going.

As they walked, Dobson, the butler, said, 'Go through to the withdrawing room, sirs. I will make sure coffee is served there.'

'Hmm.' Alasdair grimaced. 'I need to change out of my wet shoes and socks.'

'Worried about trench foot?' Sheridan commented mildly.

'Ha, many of my men had it, but I didn't succumb. I was promoted out of the trenches early enough, I suppose.'

'Yes, well I arrived late on parade. We all did, but it helped, don't you think?'

Unable to see his facial expression, Alasdair assumed from the appeal in his voice that Sheridan was sincere. He wished he could know what he looked like. He must ask Melissa. It helped him to form a picture in his mind.

'Yes, the Americans helped, if only to swell the troops in battle and increase the numbers killed.' Alasdair tried not to sound bitter.

'You don't subscribe to the evil Hun story?'

'No, evil abounds everywhere. I saw it all in my job.'

'So you were in the British Secret Service?'

'I can't say but . . . ' Alasdair let the sentence hang. There was a moment or two of silence.

'I need to talk to you. In private. Alone or with your wife.'

'With my wife in all things.'

'You are one lucky guy. Maybe later . . . ' But whatever he was about to say was interrupted by voices joining them.

Sheba's nose touched his knee, and then a hand was placed on his arm. 'Sir, I have clean, dry socks and brogues. Come with me. We can slip into another room and change them.' It was Thomas.

'Good idea. Thank you, Thomas. Quick, before they

all appear.' Alasdair had no idea where they went, but soon with towelled dry feet and fresh socks and shoes he felt better. 'So, fill me in. Before Melissa gets here. I want your account.'

'Well, what a palaver up those stairs. Still, that nurse is competent. Better than many doctors, I'd say. Mrs Gauntlet, the youngest one, once her hysterics had gone she snivelled a bit but mucked in fine. I think she is actually quite fond of the in-laws. Bit of a chip on her shoulder, though, I should think. That accent is slipping more.' He chuckled.

'Now, Miss Gauntlet. She is what I'd call a real lady, more like Mrs Charters. Polite, kind, I suspect she is the real organiser behind this house and runs the lot. Anyways, Mrs Gauntlet came round OK. She's been ordered to stay in bed. Best place for her, twittery old stick. If you know what I mean. Young Mrs Gauntlet has offered to stay with her for the time being.'

'Fondness, do you think, or a wish to stay out of it all?' Alasdair rubbed his chin.

'Bit of both, sir?'

'Good report. Well done, Thomas, have you got a grip yet on the serv . . . domestic staff?'

Thomas's grin was lost on Alasdair, but not the amusement in his voice. 'The servants' hall here is very depleted, sir. There are two maids, Betsy and Elsie – they live in. The housekeeper, Bertha Dobson, wife of the butler – she is as old as him, rather arthritic and rather deaf. There is the chef.' He must have picked up on Alasdair's twitch. 'Yes, a bloke, foreign, not sure from where yet. Apparently they like Indian food and he can cook it, but I would not have said he was from there.

There is a kitchen maid who helps him. They both live in and that's it.'

'And the chauffeur?'

'Well here is the thing, sir. He is also the handyman as well. He is the one responsible for the lighting and heating and organising the gardening and grounds. He was here last night, right enough, but no sign of him this morning. He didn't turn up for breakfast and his bed's not been slept in.'

'Done a bunk, do you think? But why? We need to investigate his disappearance pronto. Take me back to the withdrawing room. The others should all be gathered by now.'

EIGHTEEN

Melissa was sitting drinking a coffee, perched on the edge of a huge winged sofa, one of several in the room. It was covered in a vermillion tapestry-style brocade. The room itself was positively Victorian, the overall aspect a dark red. There was a huge oriental rug almost covering the wooden floor, no doubt from India. There was quite a lot of brassware, she thought, from the same continent. Various interesting idols were scattered about the room, on plinths or on occasional tables. One that particularly attracted her attention was a huge brass circle of fire with a figure dancing within it. She wondered what it was all about. She was fascinated by it all. Usually these old India types brought servants back with them but clearly not here. Why?

She realised she was rigid with tension. This was not a relaxing house, and a murder, followed by an accident, were not conducive to relaxation either, but whereas at Pennstone Manor she had felt, yes, sadness and fear, there was also exhilaration. Here, she just sensed a creeping dread. The house itself seemed to have a brooding quality, ominous and heavy, weighing her down. Or was she just being fanciful?

The door opened and in came Thomas with Alasdair and Sheba. She noticed he dropped Thomas's arm almost immediately and allowed Sheba to lead him across the room to her. This dog training was coming on.

'I am on a sofa,' she said quietly. 'If you turn around now and back up a couple of feet, you can sit down. I wouldn't flop too far, though, it might swallow you. Dobson and Elsie are serving coffee.'

'Ah, Charters. Good. Now we are mainly all here, as the new head of the household I thought I had better take charge, and we need to have a discussion.' Charles puffed up his chest and placed his feet apart in an apparent unconscious echo of his father's favourite stance.

A few moments' silence greeted the statement and then some general spluttering.

'I say, young Charles, isn't this a bit precipitate?' Roderick muttered jocularly, but his small deep-set eyes were active, moving over the company but engaging with no one.

Melissa looked around the room. She marvelled at how they all appeared so restrained. Not a red nose or eyes anywhere. It appeared that Colonel Gauntlet was not being, at least outwardly, mourned among those gathered here. He hadn't seemed to her such a bad old thing, but then she conceded that appearances frequently were deceptive. He must have done something to end up murdered, after all.

Her thoughts were interrupted by a woman she had not met before. Young, elegant and expensively understated. She looked more middle class than a governess in Melissa's eyes. Something in her body language must have communicated to Alasdair.

'Who is here?' he whispered.

'I think that was the governess just coming in. We will have to meet her later. She looks surprising. So, we have in this room Charles, Roderick, you, me, Davinia, Sheridan, Great Aunt Petunia, Captain and Elizabeth Searle. I wonder why she is not upstairs with her friend Majorie? That said, the way she is clutching her husband's arm she appears terrified,' she whispered back.

'Quite right and so should you be,' Alasdair muttered, his voice grating. 'We have a murderer in our midst and we are cut off apparently from all immediate help.' His voice had carried, despite no doubt his desire to keep it low.

'I agree with Alasdair,' Davinia said. 'This is an appalling state of affairs. What are we going to do?'

The door opened and Nurse Foote came in, catching the tail end of the conversation. She added, 'Well, the phone is out. So, no help from the police or the doctor until the floods subside.'

'Oh!' squawked Elizabeth Searle. 'Won't someone come and rescue us?'

Nurse Foote rocked back and forth on her feet, her hands pushed deep into the pockets of her uniform. 'If it's this bad up here, the surrounding villages're likely to be underwater. They'll have their own problems and health issues. And here I am, stuck here.' She sounded exasperated. 'I should be down the hill in my village. I can't do anything up here for the dead.'

'You, of course, are welcome to stay as long as necessary,' Davinia told her. It was impossible to tell from her inflection how she felt about this. 'How is Mother now?'

'Enough!' Alasdair surprised Melissa by suddenly standing up. 'Your chauffeur, Dunmore, is missing. We need to conduct a search to find him. That may tell us more about what is happening here. Every moment is vital.'

'Well, really—' began Charles.

'No, Charles,' Davinia interrupted. 'I was afraid of something like this happening. That is why I invited Alasdair and Melissa to stay. They are experienced in problem-solving. I believe they would be just as good as our local constable, if not better. I say we should put ourselves in their hands and let them investigate Daddy's death.'

NINETEEN

'Good grief, Davinia.' It was Petunia. 'You have been reading too many trashy crime novels, girl.'

'No, really, they solved a murder only last year in Brockenhurst.'

'Well, we helped,' Melissa replied with, she hoped, suitable modesty.

Charles sighed, ran his hand over his forehead and sat down with a thump in a wing chair. 'So, what do you suggest?'

'First we need to find Dunmore. At the same time, we must investigate why the phone isn't working and see if we can repair it.'

'But that was Dunmore's job. He dealt with all of it. He was more of a handyman than chauffeur,' Charles said.

'Even more reason to find him,' Sheridan muttered.

'I suggest you go in pairs and thoroughly search the house, and then the outbuildings that are not flooded.' Alasdair took command. 'Not you, Melissa, you go fetch a notebook. I am sure you brought one?' He remembered her saying that her aunt had a drawer full of them.

'Do you want to set up in Daddy's study?' Davinia seemed very enthusiastic about this. How long had her suspicions been building in her mind?

'Look, you need to understand. Melissa and I have no official standing here. If you choose to help, it is voluntary. Also, I am not an expert. Yes, I did some investigations in the war, but I had my sight then. That is why I need Melissa to help, but I must warn you, I have no magic tricks. As Petunia said . . . I may call you Petunia?' He turned to the direction of her voice, but, of course, could not see her nod of assent, so assumed it. 'This is not a detective story, but a really dangerous situation. Nurse Foote was the last to arrive before the floodwaters surrounded the property, cutting us off. Assuming that we are cut off here alone, it is essential that we know precisely who is occupying the house and what is left of the land and outbuildings. You are to be on your guard and if you know, or think you know, what is going on, for God's sake tell us.'

TWENTY

When Melissa arrived back at the drawing room with her notebook, Alasdair was still sitting on the sofa with Sheba at his feet. Otherwise the room was empty. It seemed that everyone else had taken the opportunity to join in the hunt for Dunmore, or to just disappear.

'Good,' Alasdair greeted her with. 'Thomas has given me the low-down on the domestic staff. We must make a list; it was useful last time. Can you start that? Has the governess gone?'

Gosh, he sounds like a military commander. Melissa was taken aback, but she replied, she hoped, with tact. 'Yes, we are alone.' Five minutes later, she had her list of the family through to the staff.

'Do you think Davinia's idea about using her father's study might be useful?' she asked.

'Don't you think that is a bit sleuthish? You know, like a detective novel?'

'Won't they expect that?' she pursued.

'Perhaps, but I think we do not want to be shoved into a role. We need to shake them up a bit, not conform to their expectations.'

'But do you think that will work? Last time we were bumbling about like idiots.'

'Yes, but it was us who solved the murder, don't forget.' Alasdair was frowning at her.

Melissa suddenly realised she was treading on delicate ground. He had come so far in a year. He seemed happier, less stressed, but was it all an act to please her? Had she made a terrible mistake in accepting this invitation and pitching them into danger again? 'Yes, we did. We worked well, and despite the murder it was fun. Wasn't it?'

'Yes. It was good to use my skills, those that I had thought were buried for ever.'

'So let's use them again.'

'What do you think of the American chappie? Sheridan?'

'Why? Do you suspect him? I mean he is an outsider – he cannot be involved, can he?' Melissa asked, confused.

'Well, there is something I have picked up.'

'What, you think he is not what he says he is?' She was rather incredulous.

'No, not that necessarily. Something in his voice. An over-egging of the pudding, if you know what I mean.'

'The trouble is, I don't. I can't remember if I have ever met an American before, you know, personally. So I cannot help you there. Would it help to describe him?' She paused for a moment and then began. 'He is tall – as tall as you. Well built, muscled. Fair hair, blue-eyed. Good-looking. I can see why Davinia is smitten. But not top drawer, if you know what I mean. Or not wealthy. His clothes are good enough but not the cut and quality one would expect from a gentleman. However, he must have something or Davinia would not look at him twice.'

'Well, he claims to be a veteran and seems good in a crisis. Oh, and he wants to talk to us alone. But I am still sure his accent is all over the place.'

'We've found him.' It was the man in question – Sheridan – entering the room.

'Is he . . . ?' Alasdair began.

'No, not dead, but he appears drunk and/or drugged I'd say.'

'Are you an expert on drink and drugs?' Alasdair sounded sceptical.

'In a way. Quick, before the others come. I have not been honest with you, or anyone, really. I am Sheridan Kennard, but I am not a financier. I am a Pinkerton agent. A private detective.'

TWENTY-ONE

'Ha. Told you.' Alasdair was jubilant; his senses had not failed him, nor his investigative skills. 'Why are you here?'

'Please say you are not stringing Davinia along. That would be too horrid.'

'Melissa, this is not a romance we are investigating but murder. Get a grip.' Alasdair tried not to snap.

'No, Alasdair, trust me, my intentions to Davinia are entirely honourable. I would like to take her away from all this. It is just not healthy. As soon as possible. But . . . ' As if sensing Alasdair's impatience, he raised a hand, then, realising it was wasted on him, rushed on. 'Look, I can tell you about my investigation and show you my card, but I need to tell you about Dunmore.' Seeing Alasdair nodding his head in assent, he continued, 'He was in the back of the Bentley, sprawled out unconscious. There was an empty Scotch bottle on the floor. He smelt of alcohol, but he was completely out cold. If I was asked to guess, I'd say someone knew he liked his Scotch and drugged it.'

'But why?' Melissa chanced entering the conversation.

'Because he was meant to be . . . ' Alasdair began.

'Clearing the ditch!' Melissa finished.

'My thoughts exactly. Which means in my book this murder was premeditated.' Sheridan's accent had now settled to a slower laconic drawl. 'And I'd appreciate you guys not blowing my cover.'

'Golly, absolutely, we agree, don't we, darling? How thrilling.'

Alasdair sighed. 'For now, but I would appreciate a full and honest account of why you are here . . . ' The door opened. 'As soon as you can.'

'Ah, Nurse Foote,' Melissa said.

'So where's my latest patient?' Rather than sounding put out, she seemed to be relishing the situation.

'I have left him in the garage with the butler. I suggest bringing him into the house – there is a small sitting room in the back of the house or Colonel Gauntlet's study across the hall. What do you think, Alasdair? The junior Gauntlets are kicking up a stink about having him in.'

'Yes, I agree – with a murderer on the loose he would be too vulnerable in his quarters for now, and, I think, too isolated at the back of the house. The study?' He looked towards where he had last heard Nurse Foote. 'Would you agree? Being medical can you overrule the' – he chuckled – 'junior Gauntlets?'

The now familiar intake of breath from Nurse Foote confirmed his guess of her whereabouts in the room had been correct. 'Certainly, I can overrule them.'

Alasdair recognised this as the firm tone of a former ward sister who brooked no arguments from recalcitrant patients or relations.

'I'll need a bed set up. He's not in a good way. If you are right, Mr Kennard, and I'm inclined to agree that he is drugged as well as drunk, then he needs to be watched carefully. The best thing for him would be to vomit, but as he hasn't yet, I think we just have to let the drugs take their course. Without a doctor or a hospital, there's not much I can do as I've no idea what the drug administered was. It could be poison, slow-acting, and he will die, or it could be an overdose of a sleeping draught, which could be touch and go. He will need close watching. What you need to do, Major Alasdair Charters, is find the monster in this house and quick.

'Now, Mr Kennard, if you could assist me, we'll transport Dunmore to the study. I've sent Davinia and the butler – Dobson, isn't it? – to find a camp bed or something to lay him on.'

'Actually, I think there was a huge sofa in the room already,' Melissa ventured.

'Hmm, I'll look, but a bed would be better. There's Charles Gauntlet and Roderick to help move furniture if it's not too beneath them.' Nurse Foote raised her eyebrows to show it was a joke, but then, clearly realising everyone in the room took her words at face value, shrugged. 'Come on then, Mr Kennard, let's get going.'

TWENTY-TWO

'We are alone now.' Melissa, who had been sitting with a decorous gap between them on the sofa in the drawing room, scooted along until she was as close as she could be, threw her arms about Alasdair and laid her head on his chest. He pulled her closer and they rested for a few moments in a close embrace, but it was long enough to give and receive strength, calm and comfort.

'So we have our list, what do we do now?' She pulled away and fluffed her hair.

'We will need to interview the whole household, establish where everyone was. I liked that idea we used last time of a timeline. I'd rather not use a blackboard here as I have a feeling they will all read it and then make up their stories accordingly.'

Melissa took out her notebook, came to the middle and pushed it open. The spine cracked; normally she hated doing this to a book, but this gave her a lovely double page on which she could create a timeline. 'I cannot really start this until we know when Colonel Gauntlet went out to clear the ditch.'

'Yes, and why he went ahead and began it on his own. Wasn't he suggesting quite firmly last night that Roderick help him? So what happened?'

'And more to the point, what could be the motive for killing him?' Melissa speculated.

'We need to ask a great deal of questions, and I

would dearly like to know what a Pinkerton agent is doing over here.'

'Where shall we start?' Melissa was suddenly enthused. This sleuthing might not actually be fun, but it was stimulating. Alasdair looked positively chipper. 'But promise me you will be sensible, especially with Sheba – no risks, we don't need you to have an accident – or worse.'

'Stop fussing.' But he grinned at her, his dark eyes full of mischief. 'Don't worry, you haven't been demoted. You are still are my number one bloodhound.'

'You beast.' She punched him lightly on the arm and then kissed him on the cheek. This time, he pulled her into his arms with more passionate intent. Honestly, Melissa thought when he had released her, necking at our age, an old married couple like us. Then she stopped. Well, not that old – Alasdair is still not thirty yet and I am much younger than him. She grinned to herself.

There was a slight cough and she swung towards the door and jumped up, feeling like a naughty child caught out. It was the housekeeper. She was struggling with a tray as she limped across the room. She ought to be pensioned off, not forced to work like this, Melissa thought. She dashed to her aid, took the tray and put it on a larger round table with only a small brass idol on it.

'Thought I had better provide some coffee and biscuits after the shenanigans of this morning. Luncheon will be at one o'clock.' She made as if to leave.

'Hold on a moment, Mrs Dobson, could you? It is Mrs Dobson, isn't it?'

'Yes, married to Dobson the butler nigh on forty-five years.'

Melissa found an upright wooden chair and indicated that she could sit. Mrs Dobson collapsed into the chair with a grateful smile. She was a small birdlike woman, but Melissa could see from the swelling and deformity in some of her fingers that she was a sufferer of arthritis.

'Have you been with the Gauntlets long?'

'About 1913, when they came back from India. Thought it would be a cushy job – they had four Indian servants then, and an ayah, I think they called her, for the women. Thought it would be an easy jog until we were too old to work. Got a bit put by, but it's never enough, is it?'

Melissa felt a rise of colour from her neck; she had so much and here was this elderly couple flogging themselves to death like some old donkeys.

'So what happened to all these Indian servants?' she asked. Alasdair seemed happy to let her take the lead.

'The men volunteered the minute the war broke out. Don't think they liked it down here, always shivering away and sniffles all the time. I heard they got sent back to India, to soldier out there. A lot of the local lads too.' She sniffed. 'Still, they were spared the trenches, weren't they? Weren't going to come back here after the war, were they? No chance.'

'And the ayah?'

'She died, taken off in that 'flu epidemic. Not strong, those Indian people, but then I s'pose they were not made for this 'ere country, were they?'

'Did many people die of the Spanish Influenza hereabouts?' Alasdair asked.

'Oh yes, sir, ever so many. With the men gone, women were having to work on the land just to feed themselves and pay the rents. They weren't healthy and couldn't fight it when it came.'

'So, why are there so few ser . . . domestic staff now?' Melissa almost tripped herself up in her correctness.

'Can't get good servants now. Not up here, too far out of the way. Why, you talk to Nurse Foote, miles and miles she goes on her bicycle. Where would footman or young maids go on their time off? No, they want to be in the nearest town, want proper jobs, working in shops or the factories, not out here. And look at us, with that pool of water all around. You go up to the servants' attics and have a look. Right proper surrounded, we be. We'll be lucky to have enough food. Still, that chef we've got is a right wonder worker.'

'A chef?' Melissa was astonished. 'Really, I didn't quite believe it. Out here in deepest Somerset?'

'Yes, well, I couldn't be expected to cook as well, after the last cook left and this bloke turned up. Hired on the spot he was.' She began to rub her knees and fidget. Perhaps the chair was too hard. 'Look, you have some coffee, and those biscuits. He baked them this morning, right nice they are. I can't stay chatting away here, they won't like it. But you come on down to the kitchen and we'll see you right. Find some nice scraps for the dog too.'

She stood up and Melissa could almost imagine hearing her joints creaking. She turned with her hand on the door knob. 'You watch those Gauntlets, bad 'uns the lot of them.'

TWENTY-THREE

'Well, that was dramatic.' Alasdair was fiddling with Sheba's lead. The dog trainer had recommended Sheba wear a harness and he use a semi-circular leash as they used in the war. Alasdair knew it made sense – he would be more aware of her movements and could adjust more easily – but he was loath to add anything unusual to her, to make her a conversation piece. He didn't use a white stick for the very same reason. He was sensitive to the sympathy in the voices, the conversation addressed to his wife as though he was incapable of reason. He was proud that from a distance, people would not know he was blind, and he wanted it to stay that way. Independence as far as was possible was the key to his sanity, he was convinced.

'Well, she was certainly a mine of information. I think I must drop into the kitchens for some little chats. What do you think?' Melissa's voice was light.

'Definitely. You certainly had a way with her. I am sure she could fill you in on every member of the household. Although clearly she is prejudiced, and we must watch that.' He dropped Sheba's lead.

'Well, she certainly doesn't seem to like it here or the people. Although this is a huge house and with hardly any staff it must be very hard work to keep it up. I imagine that would sour her view rather.'

'Yes, but I cannot see her as a killer, can you?'

'No, but I would really like to meet this chef. Does it not seem odd that he is the second person someone has said "just turned up"? I think I definitely need to spend some time in the kitchens.'

'But what possible reason could they have for doing so? This "just turning up"?' Alasdair frowned. 'There must be something dark underneath going on here. Something we have not grasped yet.'

'Yes, and not just the water.' Melissa looked at her watch. 'Almost twelve o'clock and I am starving. Oops and I polished off the rest of the biscuits. Where is everyone?'

'Perhaps it is time for us to make a tour of the house. I mean, we haven't seen either of the Searles to talk to, have we? Or heard them,' he added. 'Come on, let's go.' He stood up and grasped Sheba's lead.

Melissa went to take his arm.

'No, let us try something different. You walk ahead and Sheba should follow you with me behind. Sing out if there are any obstacles, though. Let us begin at the top of the house and work our way down.'

So, rather self-consciously, Melissa led the procession out into the hall and up the first flight of stairs. They continued right up, to the servants' attics, Sheba and Alasdair steady behind her. The last flight had threadbare stair carpet; the wooden stairs underneath creaked as they made their way. She stopped to check that Alasdair was all right, but he came up steadily and did not trip. At the top of the stairs the carpet stopped, with bare floorboards stretching down the landing. All the doors were shut.

Feeling very awkward, Melissa went to the far end of

the corridor; she found herself incongruously tiptoeing and jumped when she stepped normally and a floorboard groaned. She opened the first door. Unlike the highly polished mahogany door below, this was of rough pine. The room was unoccupied, a bare bed and dusty furniture. She went over to the small window, rubbing her arms; the room was freezing cold. Looking out, she saw what Mrs Dobson had described. It was impossible to tell that the house stood on a hill, for as far as she could see, craning to look through the small space, was water. There were trees poking up through the water but otherwise it was as if they had been plonked in the middle of a large lake.

'Gosh, Alasdair. Mrs Dobson was right – we really are surrounded by water. I can see the top half of trees poking through the water, but it must be very deep.'

'Enough to get a boat through, do you think?'

'Possibly, but maybe it will go down. There must be an outlet for the water. I mean, won't the rivers go down and then carry out the water from the land?'

'It might need pumps, but that would be hard, backbreaking work unless they have steam ones. Who knows? Come on, keep looking, darling, while there is no one about.'

She tried five doors. She found a tiny bathroom with a separate toilet, one bedroom used as a box room and then three occupied rooms, obviously by females. She pulled out her notebook: two parlour maids, Elsie and Betsy, and the kitchen maid, name unknown for the moment. The rooms were spartan but clean – cold, though, but with fireplaces and full coal scuttles. There were, what she recognised as, rag rugs on the floor, at least making these rooms appear more comfortable.

She came out of the rooms. There appeared nothing to see. Should she search for poison? But then how would these maids obtain such a thing? She didn't feel confident in searching their rooms, not without a witness. She paused a moment.

'What is it?' Alasdair bumped into her.

'Sorry, darling, but there is something distracting me. The end rooms are a funny shape. They go on further than the landing. Hold on, I need to check.' She quickly back-tracked to the end of the landing near the end of the house. The wall looked solid, but when she pushed on it, a panel moved in. It was a door, cleverly concealed, that led immediately and precipitously to a narrow, winding staircase.

'Phew, don't lean on the walls at the end of the corridors – they are the entrance to the servant stairs. They're incredibly steep.'

She returned to Alasdair and walked further along the landing to the head of the stairs. On the other side was an oak door with a small window in it. She tried the door and it opened.

'I think we are now going into the male servants' quarters. I bet they will be even more sparse than the women's.'

The first door on the right was set up as a sitting room with low chairs and a coffee table – a sideboard salvaged from somewhere, pine not mahogany. There were some books on it and a bottle of sherry and a cake tin. Melissa described it to Alasdair. On this floor was a woven rug, old, of Indian design, but it gave the room some feeling of warmth. There were a few prints on the walls.

'Not Dunmore, he lives in a few rooms above the garage. The chef? Doesn't sound comfy enough for the Dobsons,' Alasdair said. 'I would have thought they would be downstairs by the kitchens.'

'All right, wait here and I'll try all the others.' The room next to the chef's bedroom was occupied and Melissa recognised Thomas's case. She shut the door quickly. There was no need to pry there. All the other rooms were empty, except for the one opposite the sitting room. Feeling guilty, she opened the wardrobe. It had a few men's clothes in it. 'You are right – the chef I think.'

'Foreign-looking?'

'Why? What has Thomas said? You didn't tell me.'

'Sorry, I forgot; the chef is foreign apparently. Not Indian but can cook Indian food. Have a quick look around, see what it tells us.'

'Well, the books in the sitting room are in English, that much I checked. OK, wait, I'll have a search.' She looked for labels on the clothes. None but that was not unusual, she thought. She searched through a chest of drawers, and it was in a box in the third drawer down she found some papers. 'They are mainly in a language I don't understand. It is not French or German. Ah, here is an identity card. He is Belgian, Raoul Dufour. A refugee, do you think? One who stayed on?'

'We will have to ask him. Come on, let's try the floor below.'

TWENTY-FOUR

This time she did tuck Alasdair's arm through hers and led him to the top of the stairs, put his hand on the bannister and said, 'Stairs'. She then released his arm and went down the stairs before him and Sheba, with a small prayer that they all would not go tumbling down and land at a heap at the bottom. Melissa could feel Sheba's breath through the material of her tweed skirt as the dog followed behind her.

This landing was also divided into two wings – on the outside wall was a magnificent large stained-glass window. It almost looked too delicate to hold off the heavy rain outside pelting on its surface. Conscious of having to hurry before luncheon, Melissa did no more than give it a cursory look. She decided to keep to the same route as the floor above and turned left. Here, the landing had a carpet runner down the full length of the corridor. She walked to the end and, first of all, pushed on the seemingly flush wall. It moved.

Covered in wallpaper and cunningly concealed was a swing servant's door, complete with green baize on the reverse. She tutted but made no comment. There were only three doors each side on this floor and so she knocked on the last door on the right. There was no reply. She opened the door. Here was a large bedroom, painted a soft green with matching curtains and bedspread. It had a faintly musty smell as if it needed airing. Melissa wandered over to the dressing table; there were photos of children, an officer in uniform and a family group obviously in India from the setting. This must be the late grandmother's room, she thought. There was a door in the inner wall, and she opened it and went through.

'Golly, here is a beautiful sitting room, Alasdair. Rich coloured Indian rugs. Can you feel the softness? You can sink into the pile. They must be worth a fortune. Oh, here is her tapestry on a frame, some knitting and a pile of books on the table. I think this must be Davinia's grandmother's room. It is just as she left it.' She ran her hand across the table. 'And someone is still dusting it.'

'Her own connecting rooms, luxurious. She was a well-treasured old lady then.'

'Yes, and respected, I should think, preserving them as they are.' Melissa went over to the large window. The vista of the pool of surrounding water seemed unrelenting.

'Damned sentimentality,' came a now familiar voice, cracking with emotion. 'These are the best rooms on this floor. They should be used. Not left to become a shrine. Davinia is too emotional.'

Sheba had made a small yap and turned at her entrance, so Alasdair, forewarned, had turned to face the door. 'And you are not? She was your sister, after all.' A hint of accusation in his words?

Melissa, who had jumped at the words and spun round, watched Petunia's proud carriage slightly slump. Today, she was walking with a stick: shiny carved ebony with a bone handle.

'Don't presume to judge me, young man. I was very fond of my sister, Lavender. My twin sister. She was very good to me, and my son.'

'You must forgive me, but I need to understand this household and find a murderer.' Alasdair had softened his voice, but that appeared to be the only concession he was prepared to make. 'Tell me everything you can.'

'Well, not here. Let's leave it in peace for the moment. Come to my sitting room down the hall.'

'Whose is this room?' Melissa darted back and opened the door opposite Lavender's room. The smell of cigarettes and alcohol almost overwhelmed her; it was untidy and empty.

'My son's. Opposite this next room is the conveniences.'

Melissa opened the doors all the same. A larger, more luxurious bathroom than upstairs and a separate toilet, a fleeting impression of white enamel and mahogany.

At the end nearest the stairs, Petunia stopped and opened a door. She had caught Alasdair's free arm and was guiding him along; the dog, she ignored. Looking over her shoulder at Melissa, she gave a malicious laugh. 'My bedroom is opposite. Feel free to rummage, but put it all back, mind. I'll entertain your handsome husband.'

Melissa found herself flushing; she was sure it was an unbecoming red, but did as suggested, leaving Alasdair to cope. She opened the door to Petunia's bedroom, noting that these doors were heavier, dark moulded wood. She suspected they would be quite soundproof. Whereas Lavender's room had been exotic, this could only be described as floral. The walls were the same green, as were the curtains, but here all comparison ceased. The large bed had an eiderdown covered in a pink flowered design, the pillow cases also pink. This was reflected in the scattering of cushions about the room. The dressing table had a silver vase filled with dried flowers, as did the chest of drawers. There was a strong smell of roses, potpourri on a small table. The walls had a large print of a country garden and several small framed embroidered pieces, one of a floral bouquet featuring roses and the other was a common type featuring a house and the alphabet.

Melissa was unwilling to search too much other than a cursory look. She could not see this frail elderly woman as the killer. She might be a curmudgeon, but she could not possibly have the strength to murder the Colonel in the moat. And would she really have poisoned her twin sister?

TWENTY-FIVE

Alasdair was seated on one of two wingback chairs turned in towards the small coal fire. Petunia must be on the other, facing him. She had led him over to them and given him a choice; he chose the right-hand one, not sure if it was a test. Sheba curled in front of him closer to the fire.

'So . . . ' He heard her movement, and then a bony hand clutched his knee. 'Ask your questions.'

He found it hard not to flinch, congratulated himself on not doing so, then realised with something like pleasure that he would receive no sympathy from this woman. 'Why did you come and live here?'

'My sister's husband died nearly thirty years ago, when her son moved back to England just before the war. She was still young. Young enough, anyway, and lonely, and so I think they offered her a home here to keep an eye on things. Marjorie is daffy and inefficient and Davinia was too young to be cooped up here. So Lavender came and she stayed.

'My husband died two years ago, and she invited me to stay for a short time while the big house was being sold. I was planning to move into something much smaller, perhaps locally. We hadn't seen much of each other over the years, but we wrote regularly. I stayed on, enjoying it here. Then I made what proved to be a bad investment. So the idea of the little house went. William, her son, has always been a kind man, kind but firm. This is a massive house and they asked me to stay on. Pity, I think, for my stupidity. Pity is not much fun, is it?'

It was a spiked barb, but Alasdair chose to ignore it. 'And when did your son come to stay?'

'Last year. He left South Africa. It had turned . . . ' She paused. '. . . sour for him. He had no wife or children – that he will admit to – and he came to visit. As I said, my nephew, William, was kind, but now, on reflection, I would say he was soft.'

'Why do you say that?' Alasdair fiddled with the dog lead.

They were interrupted by Melissa coming in. 'Shall I bring another chair up?' Her jaunty, enthusiastic voice filled the room.

'No, dear, I am tired now. I want to rest. I am over eighty, after all. Go find someone else.'

'Well,' muttered Melissa as they left, 'that was a bit abrupt.'

'Yes, I think she was in danger of imparting some important information and then changed her mind.' Alasdair flipped up the glass of his Braille watch and felt for the time. 'It is still too early for luncheon. Let us carry on with our searching.'

'Yes, you can fill me in later. I ought to make notes, although I doubt you will forget.'

They crossed the head of the stairs into the other wing. Another six doors, three each side. The first on the left was the nursery sitting room. The next was the nursery playroom and school room combined. Melissa opened the door a small way and lessons seemed to be underway. The governess, who they had not met, waved her away when she looked up and saw her.

'Not welcome there for the moment,' Melissa said. 'Still, at least we know where the governess is – we just need to meet her.'

A small click indicated to Alasdair that Melissa had tried to close the door as quietly as she could.

They moved on. The last door had a pink nameplate decorated with flowers and the name Lucy. Crossing the hall, on the opposite door was a blue nameplate with a train engine painted on it and the name Robert. 'Well, at least now we have the names of the children.'

He heard knocking and frowned.

'Just checking if there are matching servant stairs this end of the house as well. Oh, yes there are. So staff can come and go at either end of the house.'

'Not just staff!' He was getting impatient now, feeling that without sight, he might be just wasting his time.

'Hang on, darling, let me just try this last room. Gosh, it must be for the governess. Golly, it is completely, pristinely tidy and ordered. Well, that is taking professionalism almost too far. There is nothing in her room to indicate anything about her. No photographs, pictures, books, nothing.'

'We must find a way to meet her and ask some questions. I am not sure how,' Alasdair said. 'However, she does seem to indulge, despite your description of her spartan room, in expensive perfume.'

'Really? I hadn't noticed. You are clever – this could be important.'

'But why important? It is just expensive perfume.'

'It would be interesting to know why she has it. Was it a present? If so, from whom and why? Does she squander her hard-earned wages on expensive things? Why? And where did she buy it? Surely not in the West Country? Did she bring it with her? In which case, everything still applies. Or is she someone down on her luck used to expensive things but now having to earn her living? Or is she pretending to be a governess? I can't think why, but Serena did give the impression last night that she hadn't checked references.'

Alasdair chuckled. 'So now who is being clever? I am leaving the governess to you.'

They went down another flight of stairs, the carpet plusher, deeper, and, as Melissa reported, nearly up to the walls either side of the stairs on this landing. This was the floor where their bedroom was situated, on the right-hand side in the guest wing. Opposite them, they knew, were the Searles. They debated in hushed voices whether to try the door and decided not to. On this corridor were all the people they were likely to meet socially downstairs. No need to beard them in their bedrooms.

'Wait, though. Let me just check on Mrs Gauntlet.'

Alasdair hated hanging on and fidgeted, patting his jacket pockets and smoothing them down. He wanted to be a man of action, not a blind man waiting, waiting, waiting, to be led and guided here and there. It had been five years now, dammit. Would he ever get used to it? He reached out and felt a wooden balustrade. It must lead up to the stairs. These bedrooms must be set back to create a small minstrels' gallery at the top of the stairs. These treads were wider, created to be a feature. Leading up to?

He turned and made his way to the back of the

landing. He reached out and found a window with a mass of leaded lights. His fingers traced the outlines of the leads. He wondered if it was brightly coloured. He remembered the church in France – half the roof had gone but still over the altar had been a beautiful rose stained-glass window. He had been distracted by it; a weak sliver of sunlight had filtered through, illuminating the colour. He had raised his hand to watch the play of the colours on his flesh, his senses drawing in the faint smell of incense, the atmosphere of reverence, that still clung to the interior despite the damage. He heard quick footsteps and then blackness. He had lifted his hand away from the window as if burnt. The stained-glass window in that church was the last thing he was to see.

He stepped back and knocked against something. With sharp reactions, he caught it. Lord it was heavy: stone. He felt around, clutching it to his chest with the other arm. There was a stone pedestal. Carefully, he placed it back on the plinth. He had no idea whether it was on the right way around, or even straight, but it felt safe. He stepped back beyond it and leant against the back wall, breathing heavily. Pulling out a handkerchief, he wiped his wet brow. A close shave that. Surprising how little things like that made him panic just like being back in the war. Still, they kept him on his toes.

He chuckled, but now he was knackered. These flashbacks still tormented him. At the time they were so real. Real and in full colour. A colour he had not seen in reality for five years. He stayed slumped against the wall, allowing his heart to stop hammering, and then he heard voices below. He cupped Sheba's muzzle to warn her to silence and listened.

TWENTY-SIX

'But why don't you think we should tell them about the tribunals?' It was a woman's voice.

'What possible use could it have? Other than to shed Father in an appalling light.'

'Better that than just us with a motive.'

'Motive? What are you blathering about, Vinny?'

'If Father was murdered, and it seems likely he was according to the nurse, then we have a very strong motive. The house, money, you get to run things how you want, I can escape. But if the tribunals are brought into it, there must be many more people with a motive.'

'But not in this house.'

'Perhaps they came and went before the worst of the flooding. I still think it is important. To tell Melissa and Alasdair.'

'For heaven's sake, he is a confounded cripple.' There was a deep sigh, then silence. 'Don't you understand? He is also a war hero. A major at, what, twenty-four years of age? What does this family have to show? Well? Only shame. I should never have listened to Father, never.'

'Alasdair, what. . . . '

Alasdair raised his forefinger to his lips to silence Melissa, but it was too late; the couple below were moving off. 'Quick, tell me who they are,' he hissed. He heard a quick movement.

'Davinia and Charles . . . but you must have

recognised their voices?'

'Yes, but I wanted visual confirmation. Just to be sure.'

'But why? You can't possibly think it was either of them.' Melissa sounded appalled.

'I don't know, but they seem to think we might suspect them.' He realised that they must be standing at the top of the stairs, perhaps too near the edge, now talking in stage whispers. 'Tell me about Marjorie Gauntlet,' he asked in a normal voice.

'She seems better, in and out of consciousness now. That must be a good sign. Mrs Searle would like me to fetch the nurse to check on her.'

'No sign of the husband? Captain Searle?' Alasdair tried very hard not to make the word 'captain' appear derogatory. How many ex-military chaps could one fit in a house? It was as bad as at his club. He had only visited a few times. Men his age behaving badly and regularly drunk, and old boys giving the impression that it was 'bad form' to come back badly injured. The word 'crippled' hovered in his mind. No wonder so many of his permanently wounded fellow officers took the so-called easy way out and shot themselves on return to good old Blighty. He felt the old rage building and began breathing deeply to calm it.

'No, perhaps he is helping downstairs?' Melissa broke into his reflections.

'Come on then, let us go down to see what is going on. Nothing good, I can imagine.'

The first stop was the study. Melissa guided Alasdair to the chair behind the desk. A day bed had been found from somewhere and Dunmore was lying on it, pale and perspiring but still breathing, she was glad to see. Nurse Foote was sitting in an upright chair pulled up close to her patient.

'He's better, breathing more deeply and evenly. The best thing would be for him to vomit.' She indicated a large ceramic bowl on the floor. Melissa cringed. 'Ha, squeamish, are you? You'll have to harden up if this sleuthing of yours is to continue.'

'Mrs Gauntlet appears to be coming around. Mrs Searle is anxious. Could you pop up and have a look?' Melissa asked. It was only sick she did not like, excusing herself. It stank so.

'I'll fetch young Mrs Gauntlet – she should be used to vomit with children.'

'Before you go, quickly tell me about these tribunals and Colonel Gauntlet,' Alasdair prompted.

'Ho, quick off the mark, aren't you? Well, he is none too popular in these parts. Good job they live so far out of the villages. I imagine there is still a lot of resentment from the country folk. Indeed, I know there is, even after all these years.'

'But what was it?' There was impatience in his voice.

'Local appeals tribunal, he was on the board – representing the military but by then it was a doctor in charge, not that it made much difference. Gauntlet had been on an early military tribunal and felt he knew who should be fit. He had a mania against shirkers, as he called them. They were getting desperate by then, of course, running out of men to send. I heard later from the doctor that they were sent targets. Numbers of men that they should try and send. Declared fit after all.'

Perhaps taking in their bemused expressions, she

added, 'Medical tribunals assessing fitness to fight. Or perhaps I should say reassessing. Of course, some young chaps wanted to go, feeling awkward being declared unfit at the start of the war, but many others were unfit and certainly weren't any better in 1917 than they were in 1914. Gauntlet said that they needed to be reassessed as the military had been kind at the beginning of the war. When they thought it would be over by Christmas? And I guess someone with flat feet might have been all right in trench warfare. Not much fun in training, though.

'Anyway, it was thought they were needed for the farming, but Gauntlet was very diligent. Some thought overly so. I heard he passed one man with heart disease against the doctor's advice. Died of a heart attack on training. That sort of thing makes you very unpopular, especially when your own son is a protected estate farmer and then, when called, gets a cushy job in London.' She sniffed. 'Still, he'd have had to do the military training, wouldn't he? Right, I can't stay here gossiping. Mrs Charters, you watch the patient.' Her eyes glittered with amusement. 'I am sure I have given you enough to talk about for now.'

TWENTY-SEVEN

'What is she talking about? Local appeals tribunals?' Melissa began.

'That would give a very strong motive to a relative of anyone who was passed fit and really wasn't and then was killed. She gave the example, didn't she? If you had a loved one whom you knew or considered was medically unfit, and Colonel Gauntlet was instrumental in getting them regraded as fit, no matter what grade they were declared, they still would have been in danger especially if they had an underlying medical condition or were in their forties. I mean, some men at, say, forty-five could be quite fit, but a bank clerk who didn't exercise? No, I agree with Nurse Foote. . . . Quick, the bowl! Turn him on his side.'

Melissa spun round. She had heard nothing. Dunmore was sweating heavily and was making small, funny noises. She turned him onto his side facing the bowl, and he then began gagging. She pulled up a chair and held up the bowl. He appeared to still be unconscious, but he was heavily sick into the bowl. She had absolutely no idea what to do. She put the bowl on the floor and rushed over to Alasdair, seizing his clean handkerchief from his top pocket. She wiped the man's mouth and laid the hanky over the bowl.

'Yuck. That was frightfully horrid. And the smell. Is there some water?' she muttered. She found a jug and a glass and tried to lift him up and make him take water, but he was not awake enough to swallow. She laid him back on his side and stepped back.

'Well done, Mellie. See? You coped. You're right, what a smell . . . alcohol.' Alasdair sniffed. 'And something else . . . '

'His dinner?' Melissa exclaimed; nursing was not her forte.

Nurse Foote popped her head round the door. 'All well? Ah, typical, just as I left, always the way.' She came into the room, lifted up the bowl, whipped off the hanky and sniffed. 'Yes, chemical. I'd hazard sleeping draught.'

'Could it possibly be self-administered?' Alasdair asked.

'You are thinking suicide?' She was silent a moment or two and put the bowl down and re-covered it with the handkerchief. 'Possible, I don't know the man well enough. So you'll have to ask him.'

'He will survive now?' Melissa asked.

The nurse felt his brow, took his temperature and checked his pulse. 'I'd say he was sleeping normally now. Until he wakes, we'll have no idea of the damage or be able to speculate as to how the sedatives got into him or, of course, where they came from.'

'You are beginning to sound like a detective,' Alasdair teased.

Nurse Foote grinned rather sheepishly. 'I am rather partial to Father Brown.'

'Gosh, so am I.' Melissa enthused, 'Have you tried—'

'Enough.' Alasdair sounded exasperated. 'When is he likely to regain consciousness?'

'Could be hours, could be a day, and even then,

he's not going to be very healthy.' Nurse Foote was all professionalism now.

'And Mrs William Gauntlet?'

'Ha, she'll spend the day in bed being fussed over and be right as rain tomorrow. It was a nasty knock, a bit of a lump, but no permanent damage, I'd say. She's fully awake now. Enjoying all the attention, no doubt.'

'Look, you seem a sensible woman, Nurse Foote. What about this flooding? Have you any idea how long it might last?' Alasdair voiced his frustration. Being cooped up here was doing no one any good.

'How long is a piece of string? This house, the waters should recede quicker than on the flat, but if it's this bad up here, then whole houses could be underwater in the villages. The farmland could be underwater for months. If you're looking for help, well, everyone will be a mite busy hereabouts.'

'We just need to get someone out with a message or to a phone. The phone here is damaged and not working. Deliberately or not, it is difficult to know at this juncture.'

'If the phone lines are damaged by the floods or the storms, then it could be a long journey to a phone. There's been the high winds as well.'

Alasdair sighed.

'Just a mo. See if they have a flatboat about the place. Not very likely. Of course, given time it may be someone'll think to come up here on one, if the floods are still high, just to check. But if the villages're flooded it could be a while.'

'So, let me get this straight.' Alasdair shifted in his seat. 'With a flat-bottomed boat, you could move around in the floodwaters?'

'Yes. One of the reed boats used on the levels. But it wouldn't be very safe. There would be a lot of submerged stuff that could wreck even the bottom of a flatboat. Also, near the rivers and streams, the flows could be fast. That's what we want, of course. The streams and rivers emptying the land.'

'But it is possible?' Alasdair persisted.

'Possible, yes, advisable, no. You'd need to know what you're doing. Local men have been reeding for centuries. Not likely that anyone here has the skills. We're much better sitting tight here until the waters recede.'

'Well, we had better be going and see what everyone else is doing. Are you fine here with your patient?'

'Yes. You go, sleuth.' Nurse Foote barely concealed her snort of amusement.

TWENTY-EIGHT

'It must be nearly lunchtime,' Melissa muttered.

'All the same, I have been sitting too long. Sometimes I think all you think about is food! Take me on a tour of this floor, won't you, darling? I need to get my bearings.'

'OK, let's start at the front door and work our way through.'

They found Serena sitting in the drawing room, working on a piece of embroidery. It was clear she had been crying. 'Oh, it's you.'

'Are you all right?' Melissa asked. 'Sitting here all on your own?' Her voice was a little tentative. She was not sure what reception she would receive.

'Yes, I am fine. I doubt I am important enough to be murdered.' Her voice sounded much more natural today. It was as if she had dropped a mask. Her voice was cultured but with the faint trace of an accent. 'I no longer have to live up to the quite considerable standards of the late Colonel Gauntlet. And what high standards they were. Come on in, sit down. We might as well talk here. There is no one to overhear us, and I may not be alone again. Respite before the storm.' She laughed. 'Literally. It has started raining again, I see.'

However, Melissa was not to be sidetracked by niceties about the weather. She let Sheba lead Alasdair to the sofa and watched them settle comfortably. Sheba was good at returning Alasdair to places she had already been. 'Am I right in saying that you are not very sorry about the Colonel's death?' she began.

'I shouldn't think anyone is, except for that harridan Petunia and her horrid son. With any luck, with the Colonel gone they can be persuaded to move on.'

'You don't like them?'

'No, she is always trying to score points, and he, well, he is definitely shifty.'

'It was on the Colonel's invitation that they came to stay?'

'Well, it began with Grandmother Lavender. She invited Petunia to stay for a bit. I think the Colonel liked Petunia's combative nature. It amused him, I think, to see us all at odds. Trapped here as we were. He held all the purse strings so tightly and we had to do what he said. You, Alasdair, must understand what it is to feel trapped. It was wearing, and exhausting, dancing to his tune.'

'But did you not realise what it would be like when you married?' Melissa persisted.

'Charles and I were in love.' Her face lit up at the memory, quite a stunning contrast to her previous attitudes. 'The negotiation we left to the Colonel. My family were in trade, carpets. My dowry was handed over. I have a small yearly allowance from an aunt but he, the Colonel, took charge of it all. Suggested we lived here. Well, Charles looked forward to helping run the estate. It is a beautiful area to live in, after all. But it is a poisonous house.'

'Why poisonous?'

'He controlled everything. You can see what Marjorie is like, sweet-natured but weak. Her vagaries, her ill health, are a way of coping or fighting back. Charles just couldn't stand up to him. He had no say in the running of the estate. That dilettante manner of his is also a shield, as was my aristocratic demeanour. Colonel Gauntlet liked it, encouraged it. Moulding us made him feel powerful, I suppose. Having to retire and lose his regiment must have been an appalling blow.'

'So why now?' It was Alasdair's turn to question. 'Why was he killed at this moment in time?'

'I think the tension had been building up for months. It was bad enough when Petunia came to stay. Two most unlikely twins, they were. It started out so well, but then all went downhill. Almost so gradually that we did not notice until it was too late. Yes, it was really when the Colonel asked Petunia to stay permanently. Grandmother Lavender was a delightful woman and a loving great-grandmother to the children. It was all so bearable when she was alive. The last straw has been the last six months since Petunia's son Roderick has come to stay. It is all too bad.'

'And Davinia?' He heard a sharp intake of breath from Melissa. He was aware he was treading on dangerous ground now; Davinia was Melissa's friend.

'Oh, don't ask me about Davinia. You talk to her direct. She escaped once, during the war. It suited him that his daughter was doing war work. But she had to come back – no money of her own she could control, I suspect. I am sure she does not want to be here, running this mausoleum for her mother.'

'And you? Do you want to be here?' Alasdair asked softly.

'I have my husband and children. It will depend

what the old man has written in his will. Nothing good, I expect. He would want to control us even in death.'

TWENTY-NINE

'Phew,' Melissa said. 'She makes it sound as if everyone has a motive.'

Alasdair was thinking of the conversation he had overheard. 'Muddying the waters perhaps. We need to talk to Sheridan Kennard and find out the terms of the will urgently. Also, if Petunia and her sister Lavender are twins, why does Petunia's son also have the name Gauntlet?'

'Perhaps she married someone else in the family? Roderick Gauntlet and William Gauntlet looked very alike. I would have assumed they were brothers.'

They began the search of the downstairs rooms. There was a music room, connected by double doors into the drawing room and French windows onto the garden. It contained a grand piano and, rather astonishingly, a harp. In this room there was a smaller kilim rug, exposing the dark parquet flooring. The room was cold with no fire. The same dark red curtains were hanging at the windows and doors.

'Well, no Indian idols in this room, but it looks like it is seldom used. I rather liked all the oriental bronzes but now they just seem sinister after the murders.'

Alasdair heard her footsteps move away. 'It is still raining, and very dark for this time of day. It makes the house very creepy.'

Alasdair laughed. 'Damp and cold I grant you, but

creepy? That is just your imagination. You describe it as though it was something out of Wilkie Collins.'

'Well' – Melissa spun round – 'you have that just right. The Moonstone. It absolutely gives the feel for this place. How frightfully clever of you.' She crossed back to him and tucked her arm through his and shivered.

'It is cold, though, and dark. I hope someone other than Dunmore knows all about the electrics and the boilers.'

'Hmm, having all your eggs in one basket. Not wise.'

Alasdair shrugged. 'Well, would you know what to do at Pennstone?'

'We have Davies, we have a gardener, and, of course, the Brigadier knows what's what.'

He was momentarily taken aback. Had she forgotten? There was no way that he wanted to stick his hands and fingers near any equipment. Then a wicked thought came to mind. 'But you are quite right – I think you should be trained up, just in case. After all, I cannot be expected to sit in the dark.'

She laughed. 'Oh you are silly. But perhaps, until we have mains power connected out to us, you could, thinking about it, be right.' She thumped him playfully. 'You do realise you didn't ask Serena her whereabouts this morning?'

'Unlikely. I hardly think she would be the type.'

'I think you are wrong there. It could have been a woman. The rake was long, with a hefty metal end. If Colonel Gauntlet was nearer the front bank with his back to the assailant, then it could easily be done with little effort. Enough to knock him out so he could be held down without struggling. Why, even an old lady could have done it.'

Alasdair blew out his cheeks. He was not convinced. That explanation required a lot of 'if's. The most important being if he had been in the right position, but he considered a fit young woman might have been able to achieve it. 'Come on. I can hear voices from the back of the house.'

They walked down the hall towards the source of the voices, Melissa stopping and opening doors as they passed. A small sitting room, a reasonable library, and then to a room where he heard a number of male voices and the crack of balls. Melissa opened the door to a fug of cigarette and cigar smoke. The billiard room.

THIRTY

Melissa placed a hand over her mouth and blinked. She hated smoke from cigarettes; cigars were all right in small doses, and she rather liked a pipe, but this cloud was ridiculous. How they could they see to play? She waved a hand in front of her face and tried not to breathe.

'Ah, the Charters, you have found us out.' Charles Gauntlet sounded almost genial this morning. Was this another member of the family who was not unhappy that his father was dead? 'I am afraid we are using the bad weather to bunk off, and our bereavement to start on the whisky.' As he spoke, his words were slightly slurred.

'Charles, just the fellow. Do you have any idea as to where your father's will might be stored?' Alasdair asked.

There was a pause before he answered. 'No idea, I s'pose it would be with his solicitor in Taunton. There may be a copy in his study.' He was picking his words carefully now.

'Would you like me to go and look for you?' Roderick Gauntlet jumped in. Rather too quickly for Alasdair's liking.

'No, that won't be necessary. You might be a beneficiary, or do you know so?'

'No, no, no,' Roderick blustered. 'Hoped, perhaps, but . . . but not expected.' He glanced around the room, with a slightly guilty air.

It was then that Melissa noticed Captain Searle sitting in the corner. They had not yet found out his first name. He was white-faced, unsmiling, and was drinking coffee. She noticed his hand shook when he raised the cup to his lips. Hangover? Grief for his old friend? She could not tell but would dearly like to question him, and soon.

'Sheridan, are you in here?' Alasdair called.

'Yes, I am here.' Melissa noticed his drink looked to be mainly soda. 'Shall I come with you? As a purely independent witness, don't you think?' He turned to Charles. 'I'll make sure he keeps it all in order.' He then turned his back on him and winked at Melissa, who, with Alasdair, was still standing in the doorway, allowing the fumes to escape and crawl their way along the hallway behind them.

She smiled and said, 'Good idea. As a businessman you should know what you are looking for.' She hoped any irony would be wasted on the men. They turned and began to make their way back to the study.

'Stop.' Alasdair halted abruptly. 'Melissa, which room was empty?'

Melissa, rocking on her heels from the abrupt halt and feeling Sheridan far too close for comfort, made a split-second decision. 'In here.' She opened the door into a small sitting room. She led the little party in. There was a small sofa and a chair. She led Alasdair and Sheba to the sofa, turned and found Sheridan sitting on a low table.

'You have the chair, ma'am.'

'Thank you, Mr Kennard, but what is the problem, Alasdair?'

'We will need to keep our voices low. We do not want

to be overheard.' As if in answer to Sheridan's raised eyebrows, he continued. 'We have already experienced Great Aunt Petunia's eavesdropping, and Nurse Foote will be in the study and she is far too astute for my liking. But we will have to make it quick. They will be gagging for us to find the will.' He turned, looking towards where he last heard Sheridan's voice, and waited.

'OK, here are the beans. I am employed by a reputable financial institution in the States to investigate a series of serious financial frauds on some of their members. After much digging, the guy supposedly perpetrating these frauds seems unlikely. He is a prestigious English merchant banker and I cannot reason why he would risk his reputation in this way.

'What is his name?' Alasdair's voice was low and even. Melissa twitched in her chair. They both knew what it would be.

'Well, obviously keep this under your hats, but his name is Bernard Lyons.'

'Yes, it will be him. I promise you. A nastier character you would find it hard to meet.' Alasdair's voice was dry, betraying none of his true feelings in relation to the man he had met on a weekend in the New Forest.

'You know of him?'

'Yes, but we haven't got time now to exchange info. Just tell me – why are you here, in this house.' Alasdair had raised his hand in emphasis.

'Other than the charming Davinia?' Seeing the black looks on both their faces, he hastily went on. 'Bernard Lyons went to the US via South Africa. He and Roderick Gauntlet left at the same time. Roderick Gauntlet is also suspected of fraudulent dealings, there in Cape Town and again here. I am certain he is intending to fully fleece his entire family. If he hasn't already.'

'But we must talk about this. Petunia said—' Melissa began.

'No, let's check for the will. It is important – even more so now.' Alasdair stood up. 'Come on, Sheba.' And Sheba began to lead him to the door.

'Allow me, Alasdair. Hang on and we will dash down the hall.' Urgency was the issue here.

They left the room and made their way smartly down the hall, not a moment too soon.

Roderick Gauntlet had his hand on the door knob of the study.

'Now, now, give us time, Major,' Sheridan Kennard admonished.

'I just wanted you to know that you may find personal financial papers in my cousin's things. I'd appreciate if you would keep these confidential. I am sure they have no bearing on the accident.' Roderick was puce in the face.

'That'll be fine, Major Gauntlet.' Sheridan Kennard's tone seemed to imply something quite other to Melissa's fancy. 'Leave it to us.' Something in Sheridan's demeanour seemed at last to impinge on Roderick's stance and he walked away, muttering something about 'whippersnappers'.

'Quick, it will be the luncheon gong soon. We must begin,' Melissa urged.

THIRTY-ONE

They entered the room, and Alasdair wondered where he could sit. Or really whether he should be here at all. Melissa was fussing around Nurse Foote. It appeared that Dunmore was still asleep but that she was happy with his future prognosis. Just then, the luncheon gong sounded.

'Look, Nurse Foote, why don't you go along for lunch. We have been tasked to look through Colonel Gauntlet's papers. I can keep an eye on the patient,' Melissa said.

'What about you, Major Charters? I can't see that you'd be much use with papers,' was the dry response from the nurse.

'Good point.' Alasdair surprised himself, as the nurse unconsciously echoed his former thoughts. 'Come, Nurse Foote, you can accompany me to lunch, and we can arrange a meal on a tray for these two searchers. OK with you, Melissa?'

Melissa nodded. 'Yes, darling,' she muttered almost as an afterthought. She was already round the other side of the desk. She looked at Sheridan. 'You take the left?' As she was solely looking for the will, she soon whisked through her side of the desk. Sheridan had pulled out a file and was sitting on the seat as he read the contents, whistling occasionally under his breath. He ignored her as she set about searching the other side of the desk. Right at the bottom, at the back of the drawer, she found a file marked "Will etc." In it was the will, discharge papers for Colonel Gauntlet and other things, which she ignored. She put the file back, having taken out the will with a flourish. Sheridan still ignored her; he was now pulling out ledgers and bank books.

'I have the will,' she said at last.

'OK, you read it and write down the bequests. I am tracking the money, if there is any left,' he muttered ominously. 'Do not share it with the family yet.'

The butler came in with two plates covered by shiny chrome domes to keep the contents warm. Melissa cleared some space at the desk.

'Gosh, I am famished.' She grabbed the cutlery and whisked off one of the domes. Under it was a fabulous-smelling lamb stew with mashed potato soaking up the gravy. She wrinkled her nose, trying to fathom the smell of unusual spices, and failed. She must talk to the chef, not just about the murder but about cooking. She had purchased the Daily Mail Cookery Book, and in it were recipes for curry. They listed using curry powder, but this smelled nothing like the curry powder she had ordered from her favourite department store in London. This was richly aromatic.

She took the plate and sat on a chair pulled up at a console table across the room. She wolfed down the meal with no regard for etiquette, glad for once to be free. She was sure the American would not notice her scooping up the last remnants of sauce with a flat fork. Bliss. She went back to the tray and picked up a jug of water and poured herself a glass. No wine for her. She was going to need her head today. Then, returning to the console table, she placed the brass idol on the floor and spread out the will. She took her notebook out of her voluminous cardigan pocket and, happily replete, with eager anticipation prepared to do battle with legalese.

THIRTY-TWO

Meanwhile, in the dining room, Alasdair could not be said to be having as much fun. When he arrived on the arm of Nurse Foote, he detected a slight flicker of consternation about the table, but then innate English rectitude took over and they were welcomed.

'Nurse Foote, oh good, you have helped out Alasdair. Come in. Dobson was just serving some casserole. Curried as usual, I'm afraid.'

'Yes, well, we can stop that now.' Charles words were still slurred.

Davinia continued as if he had not spoken. 'Find somewhere to sit. We are not being formal today in the circumstances.'

Nurse Foote guided Alasdair to a chair and moved on. Sheba went ahead and curled up under the table. Alasdair could feel her close to his feet as he sat down. He suddenly realised how Melissa normally and subtly smoothed his way. He reached out his hand and felt beyond the table setting. Yes, a water glass, but also a long-stemmed glass. He pushed it further away from him. He also, he realised, had no idea who had arrived for luncheon and who was sitting where. Until, that is, he felt a sharp dig in the ribs.

'So, been let off the leash, have you?'

Alasdair turned to face Petunia. 'Only for a short while. What shall we do? Run away together?' She laughed delightedly as he had expected. She might be a wicked old lady, but she was predictable with her caustic wit. He turned to his other side and asked, 'Can I enquire who you might be?'

'Ask away,' a deep sonorous voice intoned. 'Captain Arthur Searle, call me Arthur. Sorry we haven't met yet formally. My wife is great friends with Marjorie, and we always dance attendance when we stay.' He sounded depressed. 'Even more so now her husband is dead and she genuinely is injured.'

'Normally?' Alasdair ventured.

'She likes to play the invalid. I think it helped to cope with William. Not an easy man, and also it meant she could pass on the running of the household to others, Major.' Arthur had pitched his voice low, presumably so that others could not overhear.

'Please, call me Alasdair. Were you out in India with them?'

'Yes, William was the pukka sahib, of course. Thank God I was not in his regiment. We met regularly at the officers' club, but once Marjorie and Elizabeth, my wife, became friends, well, we had to mix more socially, and, dash it all, rank meant a great deal to William and he let you know it. He liked his whipping boys and his acolytes. It caused a lot of resentment, there and here.'

'Did you come back at the same time?' There was a pause as plates of food were put before them.

'It's casserole. Charles is right, curried.' He sighed. 'I'll give you some mashed potatoes, shall I? There you go, at least they are bland. No, they came back before the war. I think he was disappointed that his inflated idea of his skills as a tactician were not called on. Thank heavens. I was younger than him and stayed on. There were an awful lot of callow boys and borderline fit men sent to India before and during the war. I served out my commission, which completed just after the end of the war, and returned home.'

After this rather revealing speech, Arthur Searle fell silent. They both concentrated on eating their meals – a rather fiery concoction. Alasdair found himself drinking rather more water than he usually did. He had refused wine; he wanted to keep a clear head.

'Do you live near here?' Alasdair ventured after he had cleared his plate. He hoped there was something sweet to follow to clear his palate. While he had nothing against curry per se, he just wasn't used to it.

'Near enough,' Arthur replied. 'We have a nice house in Charmouth. Not some big monstrosity like this. Manageable, don't you know? Big enough for our grown-up children to visit. We have two grandchildren. They come in the summer to stay, days on the beach or out in the countryside. Nice healthy living, you understand?'

Alasdair rather thought he did. This sounded like a perfectly normal family, one very much like his own grandparents. He sighed, remembering his speculation in the train of one huge big family living in Chudley House in perfect harmony. Where had it all gone wrong? And could it be put right?

THIRTY-THREE

Meanwhile in the study, replete after her casserole and having refused the offer of fruit, Melissa was wrestling with the terms of the will. It seemed that Colonel Gauntlet had indeed tried to tie the family up just as Serena had predicted. They all inherited. That is, Marjorie, Davinia and Charles inherited an equal share in the estate, provided they lived on the estate in perpetuity. If they chose to leave the estate, then they would inherit set sums of money – presumably, she thought, much less than the value of one third of the estate. If no one wished to remain, then the estate was to be sold and the remaining money was to be donated to an Indian army charity.

She went back and made notes of the terms if no one wanted to stay. Marjorie would have £3000, Davinia would have £3000, and Charles would have £5000. She did a quick calculation. They were generous sums, but were they enough? She calculated there would be more than enough to buy a reasonable house outright and enough income to live on if they were careful. However, judging from the huffing from over her shoulder from Sheridan, she was beginning to wonder what was wrong. She turned. 'Well, Sheridan, what can you deduce from his financial papers?'

'He gave a hell of a lot of money to his cousin Roderick Gauntlet to invest,' was the laconic answer.

After some particularly sickly stewed fruit, Alasdair began to wonder what he should do next. Could he rely on Sheba getting him back to the study? He felt a hand on his shoulder and a husky voice whispered in his ear, 'Alasdair, it is Davinia. Shall I return you to the study and your lovely wife?' She giggled, her breath tickling his ear. He was not used to forward young women, but he rather liked it. So used was he to being ignored, it was something of a novelty. He gladly allowed her to tuck his hand under her elbow and lead him and Sheba from the dining room. Then, just before they approached the study, she swept them across the hall and into the small sitting room. Alasdair could only surmise that it was the same one they had briefly met Sheridan in before lunch. There was an odd smell in the room that clung to his senses and threatened to pull him back into the past. He pushed it away; it was very important that he stayed in the present.

'So what is it you want to tell me, Davinia?'

'I need to spend some time with you, explaining about my family. My father was not a bad man. Just bitter and twisted and bored. He should have stayed in India, which he loved. For him, the ideal would have been to die fighting in India or Afghanistan, anywhere but vegetating in a quiet place in England. I don't really know why they came back. Perhaps for me and Charles. Who knows? Perhaps now he is dead, Mother will tell us more.'

'Why did he buy this place and fill it up with people?'

'Yes, that is right. He did fill it up with people. People he could play with. How astute of you.'

'So why did you stay?'

'I love my mother; she is gentle and ineffective. I loved my grandmother even more. Perhaps if I had loved her less this would not have happened. Calling you in is what has set this off, isn't it?'

'It is possible.' Alasdair did not believe in beating about the bush. He homed in. 'But why kill your father?'

'What? Are you accusing me?'

The dramatic hand to the chest and the anguish in the large dove grey eyes were wasted on Alasdair. He heard the tension and denial in her voice but also a trace of something like fear. He tried again. 'Tell me about Sheridan Kennard.'

She sighed, 'Dash it, I suppose he has been talking to you. And yes, I know he is an American private detective.'

'Then why on earth did you call on us?'

'Because he wasn't interested in grandmamma. Only in this financial fraud. And I want him to succeed there. I loathe Great Aunt Petunia and her slimy son. Leeches the pair of them. That is what I don't understand. If Roderick Gauntlet were dead, I could understand it.'

Her voice rose in pitch, and then he heard snuffling. Was she crying? Alasdair hated women crying. He reached into his Harris Tweed jacket and produced a clean handkerchief. It was taken from him and he waited for her to recover. What was it about a woman's crying that affected him so? His mother certainly never cried, and his sister, as far as he knew, had never cried since she was an adult. Melissa did, but usually only for effect and sympathy, and it was never serious. Then it came to him.

There had been a woman sobbing in the church when he was blinded. He had ignored her, uncomfortable with the unrestrained emotion. He was distracted by the light from the window.

He frowned; in which case, she should have been a witness. She should have seen who whacked him over the head, detaching his retinas. Did no one pick this up? The next thing he remembered was waking in a field station, the smell of rotting flesh and disinfectant blotting out any thoughts of how he arrived there. Why had the woman just sat there and let it happen? Fear? Disinterest? Or had it been her who had crept up upon him? He rubbed his face. Why was he having these flashbacks now? Then he realised what the smell was in this room, here and now. Incense.

If Davinia was telling the truth, it was now essential to his investigations to find out what was in the will – if it existed – and to have a long chat with Sheridan Kennard. He acknowledged that the old veteran's act had pulled him in and he had relaxed his guard and trusted him. Was that how he had gained access to this house?

'Come, I am sorry to have upset you, but now it is time to find out what Melissa and Sheridan have unearthed in the study. You trust Sheridan?' He really wanted to know.

'Yes, with my life.'

THIRTY-FOUR

They entered the study together and Melissa rushed forward to lead Alasdair to a chair, Sheba immediately settling beneath it. Nurse Foote had not returned, perhaps relying on them to alert her if Dunmore appeared to take a turn for the worse. It was clear to Melissa that something had happened. Davinia was flushed and clasping her hands together. Alasdair was pale and grim.

'Sheridan, darling, how are you getting on? Charles is still drunk and probably passed out. This might be the only time I can authorise you to search. And, of course, you, Mellie.'

Melissa smiled at the pet name. 'Well, I have found a copy of the will. It is signed and dated six months ago. Presumably after your grandmother passed away. She is not mentioned in it.'

'That makes sense. She left me, Charles and his children small legacies. The rest, I believe, went to Father.'

'Well, your father's will is rather complicated and I am not sure I understand it all, but as predicted by your sister-in-law, Serena, he has tried to tie you to the house, although there are legacies in lieu if you want to leave. It depends on how much the estate is worth, how much money is left . . . Sheridan, what have you found so far?'

'It would appear that he used to invest with some

reasonable return in stocks and shares with a broker in London. However, recently he appears to have decided to invest in his cousin's schemes. To the tune I have found so far of £5000, and I can guarantee that is lost.'

'Why do you say that? Surely they might make some money?' Melissa watched Davinia's face suffuse with horror.

'If he is linked to Bernard Lyons, which I am sure he is, then the scheme he is selling is a blind pool.'

Alasdair whistled.

'You have heard of it?' Sheridan looked surprised.

'Yes, there was a spate of them around a few years ago. My father attempted to extract a few clients from such schemes. For fraud.'

'Well, I haven't a clue,' Davinia said, and she looked at Melissa who shook her head and then added for Alasdair's benefit, 'Nor me.'

'A blind pool is where investors are persuaded to invest in a project that is secret but promises wild returns for their money. Of course, it is not regulated, as no one other than the guy heading up the pool knows what is going on. If he is honest and a skilled manipulator of markets or building projects, then yeah, investors can make money, but due to the nature of the investment it is ripe for fraud,' Sheridan explained. 'No one knows where the money is going, and it is too easy to just say the money was lost.'

'And you think this is what is going on here?' Davinia began to sway. Melissa grabbed a chair and sat her on it. 'You mean that Uncle Roderick has been involved in defrauding our family?'

'Not just yours. It looks like, from the will, he invested

his mother's money as well,' Melissa said. 'There is a small bequest to her. Compensation? But it is possible that Roderick could be an innocent party, couldn't he? You know, also taken in by Bernard Lyons?'

'Not a chance,' Sheridan said. 'He was running frauds in South Africa when he met up with Bernard Lyons and then became his agent, finding investors for a fee. When he left South Africa and came to England he continued. I am sure of it.'

'What does the will say?' Alasdair asked. 'Does it look like Colonel Gauntlet was suspicious of being defrauded, as his legacy to Petunia suggests? If he was, why the hell did he not do something about it?'

Melissa recounted what she had found, and it was her turn to ask questions. 'Davinia, what do you think Charles will do?'

'You must ask him. Father's death changes everything. Serena comes from a wealthy family; they are in carpets. Her father is always urging him to come into the business, and I think he might have, until Father filled his head with delusions of grandeur. Father wanted his son to be, or appear to be, landed gentry.' Davinia turned to Sheridan. 'So is there any money left? Can we get our legacies?'

'I am not sure. From the records I have here, it will be touch and go. You need to talk to his lawyer and his investment broker. There may be other money about. But if there is, there is no evidence of it here.'

'But if they all agreed to go, couldn't they sell the estate to pay the legacies?' Melissa asked.

'Perhaps, I am no expert. Hey, Alasdair, do you know any better?'

'Not without consulting my father. Damn that the phone is out of order.'

'Is it?' Davinia jumped up from her chair and ran out to the telephone.

'However, I would say it was likely,' he continued, 'from my small knowledge of the law, but, and it is a big but, will Charles want to give up the estate? And if he doesn't and the legacies are paid, from what you are saying he would be managing this place on virtually no capital. Is it a running concern?'

'Of course it isn't! You're right, the phone is dead.' Davinia gave up tapping the plunger to call for the operator. 'If only Dunmore wasn't laid low. I bet he would have an idea on what to do with it.'

'I rather think that is the point.' Alasdair's voice was dry.

'No, I think the point is that having fleeced the family of their money,' Davinia exclaimed, 'if Roderick didn't want the fraud to come out – and Father was no fool – then he must be the murderer.'

THIRTY-FIVE

'She has a point,' Alasdair reflected later as they walked around the house, ostensibly to exercise Sheba but really to escape the family and think.

'But there is absolutely no proof that Roderick did it, though he did snatch up the tools rather quickly. Meaning, of course, his fingerprints will be all over them and he has a perfect explanation for them being there. I mean, he is not likely to confess, is he?'

'No, but we must question everyone. We haven't even met the governess yet, and we need to talk to the staff below stairs. Someone might have seen something.'

Melissa walked, thinking. She was convinced that Roderick was their man. But how to prove it? If they went to tea first – downstairs would be all tied up with that – then they could go and talk to the domestic staff, just before the major onslaught of supper preparation. Her mind flitted off to the inconsequential. Should they be wearing black? In which case, she would have to wear the same as last night. Did she have anything sombre enough for tea? What on earth would Nurse Foote wear? She had only come in her uniform. Did you invite nurses to supper? Obviously the elderly knew all the correct formalities. The elderly?

'Alasdair, Davinia's grandmother. Could there be a link there?'

'What would be the motive?' Alasdair sounded tired and frustrated.

'Well, perhaps she found out something about

Roderick and threatened to make it known to the rest of the family and had to be silenced?'

'Proof?'

'Oh, all right.' She was quiet for a while. 'But it sounds like Petunia knew she had been defrauded, doesn't it?'

'Only because it is implied in the will. He may have decided to drop that bombshell after he was dead.'

'Hmm, but if he knew it was a fraud, why did he keep Roderick on? I mean, Petunia he might have felt sorry for, although, to be honest, she isn't the very "sorry for" type and, for that matter, neither was he by the sound of it.'

'How is the water?' Alasdair asked.

'Well, it seems to me to have subsided somewhat. I am sure it was further up the drive this morning. It has, of course, stopped raining, and if you are right and someone is pumping the water out further down the hill, then the water here will drain away as well.'

'Let us hope it carries on. Where are we now, Mellie?'

'We are on a raised grassy bank above the moat. At the front of the house. Between us and the moat here is a flower border with shrubs in it. Not much else at this time of year.'

'Would the shrubs shield the murderer from the house?' Alasdair fiddled with the empty lead, having allowed Sheba to run free.

'They might . . . but not completely, I would have thought. It would be a very risky thing to do. When we go back into the house, we must check the windows. Of course, the large windows on the landings are at the back of the house, and they are stained glass anyway.'

'So does the moat go all around the house? I think

you need to talk me through the landscape. I want to understand how it could have happened. I mean, it was so risky – we were out with Sheba at that time. If our walk had only been a little shorter then we would have witnessed the murder happening.'

'Again, it is the risk that is interesting. It suggests someone who was either desperate or reckless – or both.' Melissa ventured her thoughts on psychology. For once, however, Alasdair did not poopoo it.

'You could be right. Come on, walk me back.' He called to Sheba. 'We need to be making notes.'

They negotiated their way to their room without encountering anyone else. 'Listen,' Melissa said, 'I am going to write everything we know in my notebook along with a plan of action. Why don't you have a lie down while I do it? You look exhausted.'

They had a scant hour and a half before tea. Melissa made good use of the time, writing up her notes, and Alasdair slept. She had noticed that since he came back from the war, he had the ability to sleep anywhere and at any time. She hated to think what had occasioned such a necessity. His sleep did not appear to be very relaxing. He kept turning from side to side, and she was sure he was mumbling but could not hear what he was saying. Was he having a flashback? They had seemed to have waned somewhat recently, and she felt a stab of guilt as she wondered about them coming on this weekend. It was turning into a nightmare.

She woke Alasdair with just enough time for him to change for tea, although she was pretty certain that no one would notice or find it amiss if they had not made the effort. She now had a list of questions that was essential to be answered. Where was everyone this morning at about the time of the murder? Who had sleeping draughts or access to them? And they had to interview the governess, servants and Charles.

Tea was a sombre affair. Petunia was sitting rather regally in a high-backed wing chair, dressed top to toe in funerial black, her stick an ebony cane. Davinia was sitting in a corner with Sheridan, deep in conversation. Charles looking peaky, as well he might after the drunken episode of the morning, was sitting on the sofa with Serena. No one seemed to have changed, and Melissa was thankful that Alasdair had refused to do so as well. She had acquiesced and not bothered either. She would have felt absolutely frightful in a silk day dress.

She hovered in the doorway with Alasdair's arm in hers and Sheba's nose poking out beyond his leg. No one said a word. In fact, they were ignored. Unused to this treatment as a guest, she was momentarily nonplussed. But, gathering her willpower, she entered the room and, skirting around the spare chair next to Petunia, she made for a half-moon table with two dining chairs. It was not ideal as it had a large bronze Indian female dancing figure on it. The features on the face were beautiful. But it was her well-endowed naked bosoms that caught the eye. Although not considering herself a prude, she did wonder at the appropriateness of such an object in the drawing room. She must have grimaced because something in her manner caught Charles's eye. He stood up and approached them.

'Here, let me help you.' He glanced at Serena and then Davinia. Picking up some sort of acquiescence, he continued, 'I can see you need more room. Thank heavens I can now remove all this rubbish.' He picked up the statue and placed it under the table against the wall, almost hidden from view. 'I am sure Mother will be thankful as well.' He gave a half smile, 'You know, I am not sure Mother really wanted to spend her days reminded of India.'

'But they are beautiful,' Melissa felt she had to say. There was an exoticness to them that appealed to her.

'Well, when you can leave, you are most welcome to take your pick and take one home.' Seeing she was about to prevaricate, he said, 'No, I insist. Have it as an apology for my boorishness. I feel sorry for Father being dead, but now at last I feel I can be myself.' He grinned. A genuine boyish grin with charm. 'Out of the drunken stupor arises a new man.'

He shook Alasdair's hand and clasped him on the shoulder. 'I realise that this gives me a whopping great motive, but hey ho, all I can say is that I did not murder my father. I can't expect you to believe me, but I do not envy you trying to sort this mess out. Davinia is full of surprises. However, it is not the place to discuss matters now. We must talk after tea. Ah, Nurse Foote, welcome, I want to discuss your patients.' He led the poor woman back out of the room.

'Well,' began Melissa.

'Well, indeed,' agreed Alasdair.

THIRTY-SIX

The butler Dobson, still on duty, was handing around cups of tea and small bone-china plates with finger sandwiches on them. He placed a selection on the table between them.

'Dobson, would it be a good time after tea to come down and talk to the staff?' Melissa asked.

'Of course, madam. I will let them know you are coming. I just wanted to say and check it was agreeable with you, but your valet has offered to help out. I believe he is bored, and we are overworked . . . ' He let the sentence trail.

Alasdair chuckled. 'Of course, if Charles has no objection as well. I am sure Thomas would be pleased to be helpful.'

They were disturbed at that moment by the door opening and two beautiful young children, a boy and a girl, came in followed by a rather elegant governess. Her outfit – the sensible black brogues, dark heavy stockings, black wool skirt, white blouse and long black cardigan – were all perfectly suitable, but Melissa's eye for detail and fashion picked up that these were very good quality, almost too good for the salary of a governess. It was like the perfume; something was off. They needed to talk to her as soon as possible, she thought, before examining her face. What she saw made that thought all the more urgent. She was not a beautiful woman but neither was she plain. With her dark hair in a bun and her black eyes, she could have been Spanish. But her voice when she spoke was pure public school.

'Now, children, sensible, please, remember your manners. We have guests.' She looked rather shocked when, clearly in a break with tradition, Serena swept them both onto her lap and hugged and kissed them.

She positively glowed in the presence of her children. 'Melissa,' she called. 'Come and meet the lights of my life – Rupert' – the boy shook Melissa's hand solemnly – 'and Lucy.' The little girl, younger than her brother, clung to her mother's skirts, overcome with shyness.

Melissa crouched down until she was at her level. 'Well hello, nice to meet you.' The cherub rewarded her with a gap-toothed smile and Serena, her haughtiness evaporated, smiled with maternal pleasure. Standing up, Melissa caught a fleeting flash in the governess's eyes. Something akin to triumph.

'Melissa, meet Miss Richards. She is an absolute treasure.'

The absolute treasure gave a wry smile and shook Melissa's hand. 'Call me Hazel, if that is not disturbing protocol too much, Mrs Charters.'

She may be in the nursery but she is not out of touch with the household, thought Melissa. Aloud, she said, 'Not at all. Call me Melissa and come and meet my husband, Alasdair.'

'It is a pleasure to meet you.' Hazel Richards took his hand.

Melissa was used to the effect her handsome husband had on susceptible women and affected not to notice the extended hand-holding, nor the leaning forward and then the whispering in his ear. Good heavens, what was going on?

Hazel drifted back to the children and, being dismissed by Serena, grabbed a couple of sandwiches and left the room. The children were well behaved, eating some sandwiches with enthusiasm. They then must have said something to their mother, and she rose and brought them over to see Sheba and the moment was lost. Although unused to children, Sheba royally deigned to allow herself to be petted and fussed over before they were disturbed by Thomas arriving with a platter with ready-prepared miniature scones with cream and jam. Absolute bliss. Melissa took two and damned her waistline.

Thomas gave her a cheeky wink, carefully timed to be unseen by anyone else, and then said, 'Give them fifteen minutes and then come down to the servants' hall. They are expecting you, if you please, Mrs Charters,' he added hastily, as Davinia approached.

'Going to question the servants? Good idea, although I rather think we know what happened now, don't we?' Davinia said quietly.

'It would be foolish to jump to any conclusions. There is a little thing called proof. Keep alert, just in case,' Alasdair cautioned.

'I'd second that.' Sheridan Kennard had wandered up. 'The rain has stopped, fancy some fresh air, Davy?'

Melissa watched, with trepidation, the shining face that Davinia presented to him as her answer. Melissa really hoped he was not playing with her.

'Mother is much better. She is talking about coming down for supper. I am amazed at her recovery.' Davinia flushed and took Sheridan's arm as they left.

At that point, Charles and Nurse Foote re-entered the room. Charles swiftly walked over to the sofa, picked up Lucy and began tickling her. She laughed up at him and they collapsed onto the seat with a whoosh. Petunia made a tutting noise, but at a look thrown by Charles, she turned it into a cough. With exaggerated care, she hoisted herself out of the chair and, leaning heavily on her stick, limped out of the room. The noise from the sofa increased.

Nurse Foote made a beeline for Alasdair and Melissa. Grabbing a plate from a sideboard, she piled it with sandwiches, and, Melissa was glad to see, two scones. 'Well,' she said, 'this is a household transformed and no mistake.'

'What do you mean?' Melissa played the innocent, hoping to draw her out and let her be indiscreet.

She needn't have bothered. Nurse Foote was anything but discreet. 'Well, who'd have thought removing one man would make such a difference? Shame it was murder, not natural causes. There's that Davinia with her young man. Mooning away, they are. I expect there will be an announcement soon, you mark my words. Then Charles and Serena, they're gallivanting about behaving like the good parents they should be, and so happy-looking. And Charles, I suppose I ought to call him Mr Charles now, taking control and arranging things nicely.'

'What has he been taking control of?' Alasdair could not stop himself, curiosity getting the better of him.

'He's having a room made up for me next to you. I expected to be in the attics. His wife's going to see if she has an outfit I can borrow, because I cannot stay in uniform all night. We're going to move Dunmore into Charles's father's old room.' She must have seen the look on Alasdair's face. 'No, it's all right. His mother approves. Just so I can pop in on the both of them on the same floor, so to speak. Only until he's gained consciousness. Then I suppose he'll go back to his own rooms. But I bet he gets a lock fixed now. I'd be ever so nervous. He could have died.'

'Any idea where the drugs came from?' Alasdair changed the subject abruptly.

'Ah, yes, I think so.' She leant forward conspiratorially, though there was little need; Serena and Charles seemed oblivious to anything other than their children. 'Apparently Mrs Lavender Gauntlet had them prescribed, sleeping powders. Terrible arthritis she had. Kept her awake at night something rotten.'

'But she died six months ago,' Melissa protested. 'What on earth were they doing leaving them around?'

'Well, I suppose no one thought of them as a potential murder weapon,' replied Nurse Foote, seemingly enjoying herself. 'Anyway, once Davinia told me about them, I've taken charge of what's left. They are safe in my medical bag.' With her neat quick footsteps, she moved to the chair Petunia had vacated and sat down with her plate and, giving small exclamations of encouragement, happily ate and joined in with the spoiling of the children.

Alasdair stood up. 'The servants I think, don't you?'

THIRTY-SEVEN

Standing in the great hall with Alasdair and Sheba, Melissa commented, 'It is the most amazing thing that the removal of one man could change a family so.'

'Yes,' replied Alasdair, 'I was thinking the same thing myself. Perhaps that accounts for his murder. He ruled the house too long. Yet, on the face of it, his generosity in taking in relations is admirable. We must find out, by the way, why Petunia and Roderick are also Gauntlets. Do you think the twin sisters married brothers or something?'

'Yes, you are right. I hadn't thought about it. It has been a bit of a whirlwind, hasn't it?'

Alasdair chuckled. 'In more ways than one. Come on, where is the door to the servants' hall?'

Melissa eventually found it: a small recessed knob set in the ornate wood panelling. She led Alasdair and Sheba down the plain wooden stairs to the basement. There were high clerestory windows intended to give light, but as it was now getting dark the room was very gloomy. The stairs led immediately onto the servants' hall, and most of the staff were ranged around a large scrubbed oak table with various degrees of trepidation on their faces. Mrs Dobson, however, called, 'Come in, come in, welcome.' She stood slowly. 'Now you, young man, and your dog come and sit here. The girls will get you a nice cup of tea. Mrs Charters, I'll just show you around. Follow me.'

This was not how Melissa had anticipated her questions going. She glanced at Alasdair, but his face was passive. So she moved to do Mrs Dobson's bidding. There were various doors in the long wall. The first led to a huge kitchen. Sitting at the table with his hat beside him could only be the chef, but Mrs Dobson only allowed him a cursory glance and a short wave and explanation that there was Chef Dufour.

Melissa could see that although he was dark, he clearly was European. She was suddenly desperate to question him, but Mrs Dobson had her own ideas. They left the kitchen, and through another door was a short corridor. Off this was a butler's pantry, then a housekeeper's room. Further down the corridor was a small suite of rooms that clearly were for the Dobsons. Created out of a corner of the house, they consisted of a parlour, bedroom and bathroom. Despite fires in all the grates, they smelled damp. Melissa worried about an elderly couple living in these conditions. Wouldn't it be less damp up in the attics? She said as much, but Mrs Dobson shook her head and muttered about all the stairs.

They made a right-angled turn and then there were doors to various storage rooms. Then a door with a few steps down to a room with two great boilers, a chute and a big mound of coal. Melissa looked with concern at Mrs Dobson. 'But who stokes the boilers?'

'We all do.' Mrs Dobson's voice was wry. 'Dunmore took most of the workload but he wasn't always available, like now, so we all take turns.'

'I will speak to Thomas. He will, I am sure, be happy

to help.'

'Oh, he has been useful, right enough. Lovely lad, you are lucky to have him. Nothing is too much trouble.' They left the room and went into another. Instead of a chute there were steps up to the outside. 'This is the 'lectrical machine. It's where Frank Dunmore works. It seems to be working now but it's his area of work. We don't touch it.'

'Thomas might be able to help, but it looks quite different from ours at home. I think if it is working it is probably best left well alone.' Melissa grimaced.

'It's something to do with the batteries. He loves his machine and might be cross if we mess with it.'

Melissa looked at the belt chugging around and sighed. 'But if it stops and the electric light goes, we will all be in trouble. I am not sure I fancy a trip back into the past.'

With a last look at the machine, Mrs Dobson led the way back to the servants' hall.

'What ho, Alasdair, I'm back. Thomas, have you looked at the lighting machine?'

'Yes, Mrs Charters. It's an old one, I think installed when they moved in. It uses storage batteries to power the lights, but I am not sure I would know how to keep it going.'

'Alasdair, do you know? I don't think we want to spend the rest of our time here creeping around in the dark.'

'Oh bless you, ma'am. There is no 'lectric lighting in the attics and I usually use oil lamps. There are plenty about. I'll get some out, shall I, and filled ready? Just in case.'

Melissa nodded in reply. 'How have you been getting on, Alasdair?'

'Ah, well, I have just been having an excellent cup of tea.' This resulted in an outbreak of giggling from the young maids. 'Mr Dobson has kindly given up his pantry for us to use to question everyone. Let's go and set up and then perhaps I can start with you, Mr Dobson.'

'Of course, sir. I'll give you a few moments, shall I?'

Half an hour later, they were no further than when they had started. No one had seen Colonel Gauntlet go out to clear the ditch. No one had known he was going to. They had heard about the argument last night and had assumed that Roderick Gauntlet would be doing the job. That was interesting in itself. Had the wrong man been killed? Certainly, when Melissa called to him, he had not turned round but had carried on hacking at the reeds. Had Colonel Gauntlet been killed by accident? She felt quite despondent; her lovely timeline was no further on.

Housemaids Elsie, Betsy and the kitchen maid, Flora, were all local girls. They all hated being in service in this house. They were desperate to get a job elsewhere. In Melissa's assessment, it was wishful thinking. They all seemed so young. They looked completely blank when asked about the local appeals tribunals, which Melissa thought was genuine. They were giggly young girls, not interested in their jobs particularly and very resentful of all the hard work. They especially hated that they had to muck in and stoke the boilers, especially more so now 'Frank' was laid low. So, all in all, she could find no possible motive any of them could have. With so few staff in such a huge house, it had been a bit of optimism, she supposed, to find a motive here. She had been hoping for a brother or father reassessed by Colonel Gauntlet and sent to die. She said as much to Alasdair.

He had stood up and said, 'We haven't interviewed the chef yet. Can you go and ask Dobson to fetch him?'

'Yes, of course. Do you need anything?'

'No, just standing to relieve my back. I am not used to lugging about corpses.'

'Oh, darling, can I get you anything?'

'No. Don't fuss. I am just out of shape, that is all.'

'And there was I thinking earlier how fit you looked.' She stretched up on tiptoe and kissed his cheek before pootling out of the door to find Dobson.

She had hardly had time to return and sit, ready for the interview, when the door opened and the chef was escorted in by Dobson.

He flung himself into the available chair as Dobson vacated the room and said, 'It was not me. You must believe me. Don't listen to nobody. Just because I foreigner, they no like me, but I tell you many things if I wanted!'

THIRTY-EIGHT

Remembering how touchy the cook, Mrs Smithers, could be at home, Melissa decided to leave this interview to Alasdair. She needn't have worried. The minute the chef said he had been a refugee and his English was not good, Alasdair broke into his excellent French, and the two men had a rapid conversation in that language, far too fast for Melissa to pick up other than the odd word.

It did, however, give her an opportunity to observe him. He was swarthy and dark, with a large mole over one cheek. He was running to fat, although she would have said he was no more than forty. He was quite short, with stocky legs crossed at the ankle. There was a sadness about him, something in his manner that appealed to her. He spoke volumes with his hands, his manner intense but also affected. She wondered what he was doing buried away in the country in Somerset. From the meal last night, she could tell that he was a more-than-competent chef. Was he hiding? Why hadn't he returned home with so many of his compatriots after the war? Why was he here in this particular house? As if he suddenly did not want to answer her private thoughts, he jumped up abruptly and left the room. She looked at Alasdair in surprise.

Alasdair smiled. 'He has to go and prepare the evening meal. He is excited because Madam Davinia has requested no Indian food tonight and I suspect he wants to show off. I didn't want to detain him in case he decided to poison us,' he joked, 'although he did say that if he had wanted to kill Colonel Gauntlet, the easiest way would have been through all that tedious spicy food he liked.'

'Yes, but then wouldn't he have been the first suspect?' Melissa pointed out. 'Especially as a foreigner.' She mimicked Dufour's accent.

'Maybe, maybe not. The Belgians were very welcome around here during the war. Wasn't your favourite detective a Belgian?'

'Oh yes, Poirot. Do you think Agatha Christie knew one? I must say, this weekend has been absolutely ripping for broadening my horizons. First an American and now a Belgian. It's a shame there are no more Indians left here, I would have loved to meet them.'

'Yes, well, let's concentrate on what we have. I thought you were making some notes? What do you have so far?'

'Well,' she said, flipping open her notebook, 'I think all three maids were genuine. No reason to kill Colonel Gauntlet or put Frank Dunmore out of action. In fact, I can only think of reasons why not. They need jobs, as absolutely they are not material for anything else at the moment. Far too raw. Especially at ages of about fourteen to seventeen, I would judge. And they are having to help stoke the boilers as Frank Dunmore is out of action, so even more work for them.'

'I agree.'

'Mr and Mrs Dobson. Again, much the same. They are old and quite doddery, they need the work and have been with the family for, what, nearly ten years? What could be their motive? There might be a small legacy in the will but hardly enough to murder him for.'

'Well, murders have been committed for quite small amounts of money, don't forget, but I am inclined to agree with you. Tell me what you think about the other members of the household.'

'Don't you want to go back to the study? Dunmore should have been moved by now.'

'No, here is more private. I bet Sheridan is still snooping in there, and I also don't want anyone listening at keyholes.'

Melissa laughed. 'Like Great Aunt Petunia you mean? All right, so here goes. Great Aunt Petunia, is she strong enough to wield a rake to knock out Colonel Gauntlet? What would be her motive as he provides her with a roof over her head? He has left her a small legacy, though.' Alasdair nodded and she continued, 'Her son, Roderick Gauntlet – according to Sheridan, he has fleeced the family funds to the tune of £5000.' Alasdair whistled. 'He also may have fleeced his mother first. Do you think?' Melissa added.

'Highly likely, although there is so much bad investment going on at the moment. That is why I have had to put your uncle, the Brigadier, on strict reins as far as his investments are concerned. Bernard Lyons may have made him money during the war, but it is a very different story now. Perhaps that is why he seems to have turned to swindling. So, Roderick, he has a motive, of sorts, if he thought his fraud was about to be discovered. He would be disgraced, but then it sounds like he had been up to no good in South Africa. Why not just move on? I presume he has made money out of it, commission at least.'

'Yes, well, that is what I wanted to discuss with you. What if Colonel Gauntlet was not the intended target? Think about it. Oh yes, I need to explain. When we walked past this morning and I called out, Colonel Gauntlet, as we now know it was, didn't turn. He just waved the billhook in greeting. I assumed it was Roderick – they do look alike, you know. They could almost be brothers.'

'Yes, we must find that relationship out. Why have the two sons of each twin sister got the same surname?'

'Yes, I agree, but let me think this out. Nobody seems to have much liked Colonel Gauntlet, but, as for Roderick Gauntlet, £5000 is a huge motive. Why, you could buy a whole estate of the new houses that they are building everywhere it seems.'

'But why kill him? Yes, he is a fraudulent swindler, but why not make him hand over his own money? Force him to pay it back? If he was dead, they would be guaranteed to get nothing.'

'Well, they might be worried, if they knew about the fraud, that he might fleece the family of all their money.'

'It is a bit thin. Carry on with the rest of the family. I still think,' Alasdair added forcefully, 'that he is our best suspect. Far more likely that he was covering his tracks. I wonder if he suspected that Sheridan was on to him and would share what he knew with the rest of the family. He would have to consider that his days here were definitely numbered.'

'Yes, and then he could just disappear off to look for more victims to defraud,' Melissa conceded. 'Now, Davinia. If she was wanting to murder her father, why on earth did she call us in? Is there a link to the death of her grandmother? Did the old lady have money? Who inherited it? I realise she is desperate to get away, but murder? That is rather excessive, isn't it?'

'Then the same argument could be put forth for Charles and Serena. They have even less of a motive, if they actually want to stay on here.' He stood up and Sheba jumped to her feet. 'It is essential that we talk to Charles Gauntlet as soon as possible. Preferably before he hits the whisky bottle again.'

THIRTY-NINE

As they approached the study, loud voices could be heard from within. Melissa opened the door and Alasdair was hard placed to distinguish the individual voices.

'So, did you know that there were not just only you amateur sleuths' – Charles rounded on them as they opened the door – 'but a professional American detective in our midst?' He sounded sober but furious.

'Not until this morning,' Alasdair said as they walked in.

'What else have you kept from me, Vinny?'

'I have been trying to tell you for months.' Davinia sighed and lowered her voice. 'There is something poisonous going on in this house.'

'Well, it doesn't need a genius to work that out.' Serena also lowered her voice, but her beautiful West Country accent shone through.

'Assuming it is correct, you have all heard the terms of this will. Sheridan, would you say it was all in order?' Alasdair said. In contrast, he had slightly raised his voice. He needed to take control of this situation before it got out of order.

'Yes, it is a certified copy signed by the solicitor. I assume the original is lodged with the solicitors in Taunton.'

'Charles is nodding.' Melissa interpreted the momentary silence for Alasdair.

'Sorry, old bean, do you know, I forgot for a moment. Serena and I need time to sort out what we want to do. Davinia, I am sure you will have divined, is going to leave as soon as she can. I need to talk to Mother. Decide what is to be done.'

'We are all in shock here and need to decide as a family what is to be done,' Serena added firmly. 'Charles, Davinia, let us go up and talk to your mother. You three, carry on investigating for all I care. My concern is for the living and the future of my children.' She may have released the aristocratic accent, but the autocratic air of command remained firmly in place.

'Well, that was rather forthright,' Melissa muttered to Alasdair.

He shrugged. 'It all depends on whether they decide to now work together or go all out for their own gain. Now, what have you gleaned, Sheridan? You have been in here hours. We need to be quick as dinner will soon be called.'

'Spiffing,' Melissa burst out. 'I am absolutely starving.'

'How can you be?' Alasdair rounded on her, exasperated by her interruption. 'We have been eating all day.'

'That would be the tension and the concentration,' Sheridan said. 'Sleuthing, as you Brits seem to call it, is very wearing. You need to keep your strength up, feed the body.' He chuckled and, seeing the expression on Alasdair's face, continued quickly, 'Okey dokey. So, if everyone decides to leave, there will be just enough to cover all the beneficiaries. However, if only some leave and someone wants to remain, then there will be very little left to upkeep or maintain the estate. Looking at his books, the estate was not making money. The cash, sadly, was in the land. This has been sold off in packets over the last twenty years. Colonel Gauntlet seems to have been running it as some kind of vanity project. All for show, you know? I am not sure what it would cost to make this estate viable, but you would. You run your own.'

Alasdair mentioned an average figure.

Sheridan whistled. 'Definitely not enough left. Do you think Charles will want to keep the family estate on? It is important to you guys, landed gentry, isn't it?'

'Not so much,' Melissa said slowly. 'So many of the young men who would have inherited an estate and carried on are gone or too wounded to take control. In a way, Alasdair is lucky, at least he can still manage things. But Charles . . . ' She shrugged. 'If they inherited the estate in 1913, then he would have still been a young man then, so perhaps he has no great affection for the place.'

'Depends on whether he has a particular affection for the Gauntlet name and history hereabouts,' Alasdair commented. 'After what we have heard about those appeal tribunals, I would suspect not.'

'Well, we must go up to change ready for dinner. Gosh, it is six-thirty, we need to hurry.' Melissa took Alasdair's arm and almost propelled him from the room. Sheba had been caught unawares, and there was a rather undignified tussle as she dragged on her lead.

'I can tell you this is going to be a bloody hellish meal. Be prepared for any eventuality. Keep your wits about you, Melissa. And bring your gun.'

FORTY

SATURDAY EVENING

The first gong had already sounded when Melissa and Alasdair approached the withdrawing room. The sound of raised voices could be heard, but despite Alasdair's dire predictions, they seemed to be rather jolly. Melissa had dressed in her same, safe dress as last night, as it was black. Alasdair was wearing a black tie with his evening dress, all donned in respect for a house supposedly in mourning.

When they opened the door and entered the room, Alasdair paused and muttered, 'What has changed? The area sounds different.'

'What, apart from the inappropriate joviality?' Then she stopped; she felt her mouth almost drop open. Someone had removed all of the brass idols, the Indian throws from the sofas and wall hangings from the walls. It was as if someone wanted to expunge India from the room. She had rather liked some of it and thought whoever had done it had gone rather too far. But it did lighten the room somehow. Made it less Wilkie Collins and rather more English country house. Perhaps it was this that had lightened the mood. She refused to believe that they were all this jolly just because Colonel Gauntlet was dead. Perhaps it was a hysterical reaction, the disbelief before grief set in. Either that or there was something very sinister yet to be revealed.

'Someone has removed India from the room. It has been stripped almost bare,' she murmured.

'That explains it.' Alasdair said. 'Look, let us stand this evening. Sheba will be fine. I want to be able to circulate. Who is here?'

'Better to say who is not. Roderick is not here. Nurse Foote is not here. Oh, but the governess is. Ah, Dobson, yes, two sherries please. Come on, Alasdair, let us go and talk to her.'

Just as they were crossing the room, Melissa picking her way cautiously, there was a collective intake of breath and someone began muted clapping.

'Oh, well done, Mother.' Davinia stilled her gloved hands and went across and kissed her on the cheek. She kissed Elizabeth Searle and Captain Searle as well, as they seemed to be a kind of rear guard for Marjorie.

'Well, Nurse Foote said I could venture down. I mustn't get too tired, must I, Elizabeth?'

Her friend smiled warmly down at her. 'No, of course not, but it is good to be with the family now.' She gave a small shiver and caught her husband's hand. 'Safety in numbers, don't you think, Arthur?' She looked around as if apologetically. 'This is such a huge house after all.'

'I agree, this is far too big to be managed now. We are in different times,' Marjorie began.

'Very different times,' agreed Serena.

Melissa was unsure whether they were referring to the era or the death of the Colonel.

'Where is Charles?' whispered Alasdair.

'To your left, beside Serena, and he looks sober,'

Melissa added.

'So, Charles, have you had time to absorb all of this new information?' Alasdair began. 'Is this the moment, now everyone is gathered, to discuss things out in the open?'

'Oh yes, we have.' Serena was like a lioness defending her brood. 'We will not be ruled by an old man who is dead. We will be leaving just as soon as we can. We want the children to grow up in this century. Somewhere small, manageable and homely.'

Petunia cleared her throat; this evening she was sitting again in an upright chair, iridescent with jet. 'Your father has been most generous to me.' Her voice seemed to tremble. 'And I am sure you will be thrilled to learn that as soon as it can be arranged, I shall retire to somewhere suitable.'

'And I shall be looking for somewhere in Charmouth, near my dear friends.' Marjorie sighed. 'William and I felt we had no choice when he inherited this house. He really did want to make it work. A large family home for us all. But somehow, I am sorry, dears, it became a cage. I know you felt your father was harsh, but he desperately wanted to bring this house to life, to be a family. Charles, you have no idea how hard it was to send you away to England to school. It broke my heart.'

Charles moved over to take his mother's hand.

'I feel making you come here was his way of indulging me. I so much wanted to get to know you, but his expectations were too high. I never wanted you to be unhappy, dear boy.'

Tears had gathered in her eyes, and there were tears being shed elsewhere as well.

More melodrama, Melissa thought, brushing her eyes with her gloved hand. Then, remembering her makeup, she tutted, but then blessed that she had black elbow-length gloves on and the smears did not show. Too often she had ruined perfectly good pairs of white gloves by wiping her eyes.

'So, what happens now?' Charles asked. 'Davinia, what have you decided to do?'

Davinia coloured prettily. She was dressed in a grey that brought out the colour in her eyes. 'Well, we have an announcement. Sheridan and I are engaged. I will be going with Sheridan when he returns to the States.'

There was a sharp intake of breath and murmurs of congratulation. Melissa schooled her face to be bland as she went over and kissed Davinia in congratulation, but inside her mind was racing. She wanted to run out of the door and take Alasdair with her and talk and talk. Was it only she who thought this whole situation was peculiar? There had been a murder in the house. Had they forgotten? Perhaps two, if one included the grandmother, Lavender Gauntlet. In her confusion, she accepted another round of sherry. She made her way back to Alasdair, who was chatting to Hazel Richards, but as she approached, she was intercepted by Serena.

'Please don't think us uncaring. We are only too aware of the situation. Marjorie is right – we resented William Gauntlet terribly, but Charles loved his father underneath it all and he recognised what his father was trying to do. But after the war, everything had changed. We had changed. We didn't want to be moulded into the image he had created for us.'

The second gong sounded. Melissa made her way to

Alasdair's side and he turned towards her. 'Saved by the gong,' he muttered into her ear.

FORTY-ONE

They made their way into the dining room. Sadly, it was as gloomy as before, although it appeared that the rain outside had abated. Dobson had switched on the electric standard lamps, as without them it was difficult to see. However, they seemed to be flickering in what seemed to Melissa an alarming fashion. Thomas was helping Dobson serve that evening with Elsie standing in the background. Because of this, Alasdair's place setting was perfect. Sheba disappeared under the table and hunkered down out of the way.

The configuration of the table was very different this evening, as Melissa explained it to Alasdair. Marjorie was still at the end of the table as last night, flanked again by Arthur and Elizabeth Searle. At the head was Charles, as the new head of the family. He had Serena on his right with Melissa on his left. Alasdair was seated next to Melissa with Petunia on his left. She seemed rather subdued that evening, although, forewarned, Alasdair was prepared for bony elbows in the ribs. Perhaps her mood was affected by the fact that the place next to her was empty. When Melissa enquired of Charles, he gave her to understand that Uncle Roderick was indisposed. Davinia mouthed 'Drunk' across the table. Perhaps she then felt guilty because Petunia could not have failed to miss her explanation of the absence, and she called over Elsie.

'Elsie,' Davinia said, 'go and see if Nurse Foote wishes to join us. She must be able to leave Dunmore now, and it seems we have a spare place.'

Melissa continued describing the seating plan. Sheridan was opposite him next to Serena with his new fiancée, Davinia, beside him. Next to Davinia was the unknown, at least to Melissa, governess, Hazel Richards. She realised there were a number of conversations that she had missed and was keen to catch up with Alasdair.

It seemed to her that everyone about the table had forgotten that Colonel Gauntlet had been murdered. Had they collectively decided it was Roderick Gauntlet who was guilty and so could relax because he was not there? Was that why he was not here? Was he guilty and was staying away, or was he staying away because he realised he was number one suspect? What, as a family, would they do about that? What about the missing money?

Alasdair played on the stock market with firm advice from his broker; sometimes he made good gains but there were always losses. These had to be offset, but Alasdair's policy always seemed to be not to cry over spilt milk. The amounts of money he invested were a paltry sum compared to the amount that Roderick Gauntlet had defrauded the family out of. She wondered if it was true that he had also fleeced his mother. From the will, it would certainly seem that William Gauntlet felt some responsibility towards his aunt. Had he regretted asking his cousin to stay? They still had no idea about the background of this immediate family and the undercurrents lying beneath the surface. No wonder Petunia was so quiet this evening.

The door opened and Elsie ushered in Nurse Foote. She had removed her apron and cap but was still in her navy surge dress. 'I thought you'd rather I hurried so dinner could be served rather than wait for me to change,' Nurse Foote said apologetically as she was ushered to the seat between Petunia and Arthur Searle.

The first course of soup arrived almost immediately. It was the bright red of tinned tomato soup, but when Melissa savoured her first spoonful she almost groaned with pleasure. The chef may have been running out of fresh food, but he clearly was extremely talented. He had added some herbs and something creamy to it that raised the tinned soup to almost perfection. There were gasps around the table.

'Golly, this soup is absolutely spiffing, Davinia,' Melissa said.

'Well, we felt a change from all the curry would be welcome. The fresh food is running out so I asked chef to be creative. I must say, if this is what he creates from tinned soup, I am looking forward to the rest of the meal.'

'How on earth did you acquire such a paragon? He could grace a top hotel if this is anything to go on.' Melissa laid down her spoon with a satisfied smile.

'Well, it was the most extraordinary piece of luck. He turned up one day about a year ago and said he wanted to settle in the area. I am afraid I did not question him too closely – he offered to cook us a meal in place of references and once we had tasted it . . . well, would you have turned him away?'

'Absolutely not,' Melissa agreed. 'With the shortage of men after the war, a male chef was indeed a catch.'

'He came to look for his brother,' Alasdair cut into the conversation. 'Did you know that?'

'What? How extraordinary. He said nothing to me.' Davinia looked around at the rest of the family, who shook their heads.

'They are shaking their heads,' Melissa murmured to Alasdair.

'He came looking for his dead brother,' Petunia corrected. Her voice crackled with venom. 'He was a refugee from the war in Belgium. His brother ended up hereabouts, became a farm worker.' Her dark eyes flashed around the table as if seeking reactions. Melissa did the same. This was news to her, but then she had not followed the rapid conversation with Raoul Dufour, nor had Alasdair had time to tell her the gist of it.

'How do you know this, Aunt?' Davinia exclaimed.

'I pay attention, and he used to talk to Lavender. She made it her business to be kind, caring and interested in people. She told me about him. It made an interesting story.' Petunia laughed, but there was very little humour in it.

The soup bowls were whisked away and replaced with a delicious mousse. It must have been made once again with canned fish, but he had added some fresh savoury vegetables and herbs to create a great flavour.

There was a lull while the company savoured the delicious food.

'Yes,' Petunia continued, 'he was looking to discover what had happened to his brother. You were quite right, Melissa. The chef worked in a London hotel when he arrived in England from Belgium. His brother got separated and was billeted down here in Somerset.'

She paused to have a drink from her wine glass. 'Shall I continue, or is this not a suitable conversation for at table?' Her glance this time was sly.

There was again an awkward silence, interrupted by the delivery of a stunning Boeuf Wellington. The pastry was crisp, the pate rich, and the fillet of beef was juicy, pink and tender. Gosh, thought Melissa, the chef really is pulling out all the stops tonight. She picked up her cutlery in anticipation and tucked in.

'If you have something to say, Great Aunt, then please do. This family has nothing to hide.' Charles finally broke the silence, glaring at his great aunt as if daring her to continue.

'Are you sure about that?' Petunia muttered under her breath, but not so low that Alasdair, sitting next to her, couldn't hear it.

'His brother applied to join the army when he arrived,' Alasdair said. 'He wanted to do his bit, having seen what the Bosch did to Belgium. But he had weak lungs due to a childhood illness. He may have been able to work on the land, but only if he paced himself. A local appeals tribunal declared him fit in 1918. He did not survive.' Alasdair's delivery was brutal.

There was an uncomfortable silence around the table.

'So you think . . .?' Sheridan was on the ball, Melissa could see.

'Well, I think he may have left it rather long to kill Colonel Gauntlet and poison the rest of us. Don't you agree?' Alasdair grinned as he lifted a delicate morsel with his fork and popped it into his mouth.

FORTY-TWO

There was a clatter as various eating irons were put down in a hurry. Alasdair chuckled. He had had his fun and a little bit of payback. He was not sure what Petunia was playing at, but he was quite sure that Raoul Dufour was not the murderer. Roderick Gauntlet might not be the only one who was fleecing Colonel William Gauntlet, but as Sheridan seemed not to have picked that up, Alasdair was not going to enlighten them now. He had a great deal of sympathy for unfit men sent to the trenches. How much was a brother worth?

'Oh, Charles, do you think he has poisoned us?' Marjorie wailed and she clutched Elizabeth Searle's hand. Alasdair could imagine their combined looks of horror.

'Don't be silly, Mother. Alasdair is right. Why do it now? He must have known for a very long time if it was Father who caused his brother's death.' Charles spoke sharply.

Alasdair nodded his head in confirmation. He might never like Charles Gauntlet, but he was prepared to let him win his respect. If he tried hard enough.

'Well, I cannot wait to leave this awful place. I hated the heat in India and now how I hate the damp here. I am going to look for a nice little comfortable house by the sea. As soon as the flood has subsided, I shall be leaving with Elizabeth and Arthur,' Marjorie stated firmly.

'We shall need to stay on to complete all the legal details. We shall also need to unpick the finances.' Charles paused, and Alasdair wondered what had transpired.

Sheridan replied, 'I shall, of course, continue if you want me. As I shall now be joining the family, I can assure you I will be very diligent.'

'I am sure you will. However, we must remember that Father may have made another will. Although I think that is unlikely,' Charles returned.

Alasdair thought this was all most interesting. They seemed to have forgotten that there were strangers present. Himself and Melissa, Hazel Richards and also Nurse Foote. Was there something here that he had missed? Was every person in this room in some kind of conspiracy together? Or was he just over-thinking the whole thing? Certainly there were an awful lot of people in this house who had to gain from Colonel Gauntlet's death.

It was then that Marjorie Gauntlet dropped her bombshell. 'I am so pleased you have been able to join us for dinner, Nurse Foote. Your standard of medical care is exemplary. I do so want to thank you. You have been so kind over the years. I must say, it was a very good job that you arrived after the flood. The way that you used to go on about the tribunals to William, one might have thought you could have had a motive to kill him yourself.'

'So you do take notice of what's going on around you after all?' Nurse Foote said wryly. 'Well, yes, I did have an interest in what William Gauntlet did in the tribunals. You probably don't know that the doctor on those tribunals at the end of the war was a young man who I was very fond of. We'd an understanding. He despaired of what was happening but wasn't strong enough to stand up to Colonel Gauntlet.'

'Very few people were,' Charles said, his tone depressed.

'Well, Doctor Beamish was very conscientious. After the war, he tried to trace those men whom he felt should not have been sent. To follow them up. Depressingly few of them survived, as the local villagers can attest. They were no "thankful villages". Not all the men came back.' She sighed.

'What happened, my dear?' Arthur Searle asked. His voice had the stain of sympathy that Alasdair hated. It did, however, seem to work on Nurse Foote. There was another long sigh.

'He killed himself. A shooting accident it was called, to be kind to his family, but I knew. He was eaten up with remorse and couldn't cope with the fact that he who'd dedicated himself to preserving life should have been responsible for taking it. Unlike' – her voice became cold – 'Colonel Gauntlet. I too am dedicated to preserving life, but it doesn't mean I couldn't make a life uncomfortable. And that was all. He had a thick hide, your husband.' She paused and Alasdair again missed any visual clues. 'But I was persevering. He would've got the point eventually. The murderer has deprived me of my small acts of revenge.'

'But equally, Nurse Foote, you might have become tired of the baiting and decided to up the punishment?' Alasdair asked quietly.

It was at that point that the lights decided to fail.

FORTY-THREE

The room was cast into deep shadow with only the candles on the table creating any light. Marjorie Gauntlet stood up in a rush, flapping her arms around, knocking the table and creating a draft that blew out the candles in the candelabra nearest her.

'What is happening?' Alasdair asked Melissa quietly.

'The lights have failed, and Marjorie has succeeded in extinguishing one of only two candelabra. The room is in virtual darkness.'

'Thomas, are you here?' Alasdair called. 'Come on, we need to go and check the electrical system.'

'Don't take the light,' wailed Marjorie.

Alasdair turned and said, 'Light is one thing I do not need. Come, Sheba, Thomas, follow on.'

'Well, as an exit line, that sure was a humdinger.' Sheridan laughed. 'Should I go and attempt to give them a hand?'

'No!' Melissa and Davinia spoke at once together. Davinia looked slightly chagrined at her outburst and added, 'Will they be all right?'

'Oh yes, Alasdair will be in his element, and I am sure that Thomas knows precisely where an oil lamp is available.' Melissa's voice was cool, hiding her palpitations at the risk Alasdair was taking.

'But perhaps I should go?' Charles sounded dubious.

'We must all stay together,' Melissa said, 'Surely,

Sheridan, you can see the sense in that?' She gave him what she hoped was a significant look.

'But the children!' It was Serena's turn to wail.

Melissa rubbed her temples. All these histrionics were getting rather wearing, and she felt the beginning of an incipient headache.

Hazel Richards, who had stood and was relighting the second candelabra from a candle from the first, turned to her employer and said, 'They will be fast asleep. It would not be kind to wake them. They have the oil nightlights on the wall in each room, after all. I lit them before I came down. Best not to disturb them.' Her voice was firm. Serena subsided.

They sat around in the subdued candlelight, everyone appearing unwilling to catch each other's eye. There was silence, other than the crackle from the fire. Melissa began to finish her plate. The beef had been so good. The wind and rain had abated. She did hope that meant that the waters would recede soon, and she was just about to say anything to break the tension when the door opened and Dobson came in bearing two oil lamps.

'There may be a slight delay in the rest of dinner, sir.' He addressed Charles.

'Have you any more of those?' Nurse Foote asked. 'I really ought to check on my patient.'

'And I would like to check on the children.' Serena had regained her confidence.

'I can do that, Mrs Gauntlet,' Hazel Richards said.

'No, I need to see them for myself. Thank you all the same.'

From the shocked look that Hazel Richards threw

Serena, Melissa gathered that gratitude had been a sentiment rather in short supply in Serena's vocabulary, at least to the governess. Was it advisable for the group to disperse? She was at a loss as to how to communicate her worries to them without causing more hysterics. There was still a murderer about and, if it wasn't Roderick Gauntlet, then it was highly likely that person was in the room with them.

They waited. Serena returned and, thankfully, with the second oil lamp that she had taken to light her way. The children were fast asleep as predicted. She said that Nurse Foote had decided to stay with her patient. Hiding, more like, Melissa thought. Here was yet another person with a motive to kill Colonel William Gauntlet.

Hazel, who had been hovering close to the door, anxious about her charges, Melissa assumed, made to move back to her chair. At that moment there was a terrific thumping. It sounded as if something – or someone – was falling down the stairs. Melissa jumped up, but Hazel was out of the door before anyone could stop her.

'No, don't go, stay here,' Marjorie wailed, as she saw others clearly about to exit the room.

'I agree,' Sheridan said. 'You're right, Melissa, the family should stick together. We have no idea who killed Colonel Gauntlet and there is no point giving anyone lone targets. Let's sit in the light and wait for it all to pan out.'

Thus it was that Alasdair, successfully negotiating up the servant stairs with Sheba, having left Thomas trying to start the motor of the electric system, was witness to an extraordinary confrontation on the main staircase.

'What's . . . what's happening? Who switched off the lights?' It was the slurred voice of Roderick Gauntlet. 'What are you doing? Trying to kill me? I fell down the bloody stairs. Bring me a light, girlie. I'll not sit in the dark.'

'That is where you deserve to be.' It sounded like the governess, Hazel Richards. But Alasdair was confused by her harsh colonial accent. 'You are nothing but a disgusting dronkie. Never forget, I know just who – and what – you are.' The words were venomous and the accent suddenly strong.

Alasdair paused on the top step, his hand on the slightly open baize-backed door of the servants' quarters. So, there was a South African connection here. Had he been a confounded fool? Melissa had muttered at one point about whether the wrong cousin had been killed. Had Roderick Gauntlet been the intended target all along? Had this bland, absolute treasure of a governess hidden a murderess?'

'Why, God bless you, sir. What are you doing standing there and with your dog too?' Mrs Dobson's voice cut into his thoughts as she mounted the stairs behind him. So intense had been his concentration on the scene on the stairs above, he had not noticed her ascent behind him. He was forced to carry on through the door and reveal himself.

'Here, woman, ignore him, give me that light,' Roderick Gauntlet snarled.

'But, sir,' Mrs Dobson began.

'Give it to him. Otherwise we will have a fight on our hands,' Alasdair said.

There were lurching footsteps across the hall and

then the thumping footsteps of Roderick Gauntlet returning up the stairs. Alasdair just hoped he would not trip and set fire to the place on his way. Someone would have to check on him later, if only for their own safety from conflagration.

'But what do we do now, sir? It's pitch black. I'd brought up the light for the hall.'

'Who else is here?' Alasdair muttered.

'Why, no one, sir? Who did you expect?'

'Don't worry, I must have imagined it.' Alasdair did not want to alert the governess if she was still skulking about. But he also thought he had heard a second set of footsteps as well as those of the governess. 'I must have been mistaken. He must have been talking to himself. Come, take my arm, I can get us safely to the dining room at least.'

They had just entered the room when Thomas came up behind them, all of a fluster. 'I have got the motor running but it seems to make no difference to the lights. Perhaps if the batteries are fully discharged the motor takes a while to charge them. Sorry, does anyone here know?' He seemed to address the room.

'I think that may be right,' Marjorie wavered. 'It happened once before. It took hours for them to come back on. That is why I panicked earlier. It is important to keep the motor running. Oh, why did no one listen to me? You heard me last night. I hate the darkness. Why did no one else learn it? Oh, I am so frightened!' Hysteria clearly threatened.

Davinia walked over to her mother, put her arms around her and said, 'Come, Mother. I know this has all been terribly upsetting but try and remain calm. I will sleep with you this evening. You will not be alone.'

FORTY-FOUR

'What has been happening?' Alasdair hissed to Melissa. His face had that look on it when she just knew he had found out something significant.

'Serena has been upstairs and checked on the children. All is well and she is safely back. Miss Richards went out, I presume to hear the cause of all that thumping.' She looked expectantly at Alasdair, then cursed her idiocy. 'Do you know what it was?'

'Roderick Gauntlet.' Alasdair kept it short.

Melissa suddenly realised that he did not want to reveal too much to the company present. 'Well, Miss Richards is back but Nurse Foote went to check on her patient and has not returned.' She had a sudden thought. 'How did she cope without a light?'

'Oh, she had a small torch in her pocket,' Serena said. 'Always prepared is Nurse Foote. There was already a lamp burning in Dunmore's room. We had some fixed on the walls in the main bedrooms just in case. And, of course, I had a lamp, and we went up together. She was certainly safe when I left her.'

As if suddenly reminded, Alasdair said, 'Someone will need to check on Roderick Gauntlet. He is as drunk as a lord and has taken a lamp. I wouldn't put it past him to set light to the place, the state he is in.'

'Please, can we take one of the lamps for the hall? We need light there.' Mrs Dobson was attempting to swoosh her husband out of the door.

'Yes, of course, Mrs Dobson.' Davinia was back in her organisational character. 'Look, Dobson, wait, arrange for oil lamps about the place, oh, and candles for everyone. May I suggest we abandon dinner after we have all finished this course and go to bed early tonight? There are spare oil lamps in every bedroom. We liked to be prepared.' She gave a faint smile.

'I think you will find Thomas will have anticipated this. That is where he has gone, I don't doubt,' Alasdair speculated. 'Do you need a candle, Melissa? I certainly don't need one.'

He sounded smug. In his element, Melissa thought rather belligerently. 'Well, I need a holder for it at least,' she muttered, and then, watching his face fall, felt rotten. 'Look, don't worry, I can use a plate. Hope you don't mind, Davinia?' she said as she dropped some wax from one of the candles onto a side plate and stuck the candle in it.

'How very practical of you.' Davinia chuckled. 'I suggest we all follow suit. Come on, Mother, let's get you to bed.'

The rest of the arrangements were lost to Melissa as she smartly negotiated out of the room with a set expression of wry indulgence, following Alasdair and Sheba, who had gone on ahead.

Thomas was waiting for them in the hall. He had a lamp in his hands. 'Here, madam, no need to concern yourself with a candle. I'll see you up with this lamp.'

Melissa smiled; he had the sense not to disturb Alasdair, and, to be fair, her candle did seem a bit wobbly on the plate. She had not thought to pack her torch with her gun in her handbag that evening. 'Do you have matches?' she enquired. 'Just in case of anything going bump in the night?'

Thomas shook the box of matches and led the way. Once they were in the bedroom, he put his lamp on a high dresser and began to trim and light their oil lamp. The fire was lit and Melissa knew whom she had to thank for that. Thomas cosseted them very well.

'Any news?' Alasdair was terse. Melissa looked at him in surprise. He had sat at one of the wooden upright chairs. Sheba had retired to her blanket in the corner.

'Well, the chef, Raoul Dufour, has the right wind up. I think he got so carried away with chatting to you, sir, in fluent French that he forgot he was giving himself a blooming great motive.'

'And?'

'Well, he says he likes it here, quiet and not too stressful, but on a little bit of pressure, like, he admitted he was hoping for a handout. Compensation for his brother, like.'

'But that is even more of a motive?' Melissa burst out.

'Only if he already has the handout. What does he want it for?' Alasdair sounded on a more even keel now. Melissa was always forgetting how tired he became, especially when they were in a strange house and sleuthing. Funnily enough, now they were so close to a solution, she only felt exhilaration.

'He wants to open a little restaurant on the south coast. He says that working in a big London hotel is a mug's game, as is service.'

'Oh, perhaps he could open a restaurant near us?

His food is delish.'

'That would be food dished up by a blackmailer at the very least,' Alasdair muttered drily. 'What do you think, Thomas?'

'As to the restaurant, great idea, but I think he is underestimating the work involved.' Then he must have registered the look on Alasdair's face and decided it was clearly not the time for humour. 'Despite the hoped windfall, I think he is on the level. He clearly adored his younger brother and had been protective of him all his life. I think he blames himself for not searching harder for him. I have had a quick ask around of the staff, and when the Colonel was killed, he would have been at work in the kitchen with Dora the kitchen maid, and all of us were in and out. It would have been a hard thing to achieve for him, I'd say.'

'Yes, on reflection, and to use your psychology, Melissa, this murder required a huge amount of daring and luck. What if someone had been looking from one of the front upstairs windows? They would have witnessed the murder. In fact, now I think about it, it seems extraordinary that no one saw anything.'

'We are sure it was murder aren't we, sir, madam?'

'Well, he didn't hit himself on the back of the head,' Alasdair exploded.

'But, hey, wait a moment. We only have Nurse Foote's word that it was murder. What if she is lying?' Melissa was happy to explore this option.

'Or worse still. What if she is the murderess, as Marjorie Gauntlet suggested?' Alasdair dropped in.

FORTY-FIVE

'No, I cannot believe that. I like her.' Melissa protested.

'So do I,' Alasdair admitted with a sigh. Then, remembering that Thomas must still be standing there, 'Anything else, Thomas? You must be shattered.'

'Ah, I am all right, sir. The maids are all of a twitter. Like old servant quarters, there are no locks on the door of the bedrooms. I have taught them the old chair under the doorknob trick. That seemed to calm them.' He moved quickly, his footsteps muted on the rug. 'You are safe here. You have locks on all the doors. I've locked the bathroom door on Nurse Foote's side and have taken the key. Here, madam, keep it safe. I have also locked the outer bathroom door from within. No one can now enter without you letting them. Oh and lock the bedroom door after I've left. Wait a mo. Do you fancy some cocoa?' Seeing Melissa's face, he added, 'I'm making some for myself. It is no trouble. Really it isn't.'

'That would be spiffing, Thomas.' Melissa grinned at him. 'Oh and if you should find some brandy that would also be welcome!'

'Righty ho. Now lock the door.'

'He is right, you know,' Alasdair said. 'It is no good you giggling. There is a murderer here and we need to go through everyone with a fine-tooth comb. Then we need to plan how to expose the person we think it is.'

Melissa got out her notebook. 'Let us go through everyone in the house and see what we have.'

'What about the servants? Let us start with the most unlikely and move on.'

Melissa began writing. 'The maids. Elsie, Betsy and Flora.'

'I can think of no possible motive. Other than the Colonel was possibly a hard taskmaster and that in a house this size they must have had an almost criminal amount of work to do,' Alasdair commented. 'They may have lied about a connection to the tribunals, but is it not likely that they would know what each of them were up to and could provide alibis for the time of the murder?'

'Actually, Alasdair, I would think it was the exact opposite with a house this size with only two upstairs maids, an arthritic housekeeper and an elderly butler. They could have spent plenty of time avoiding each other. There are two sets of back stairs for a start.'

'Oh good grief, this is almost impossible. Let us discount them for the moment.'

'Are you including Mr and Mrs Dobson in that?' Melissa asked.

'I would have said she was too infirm. Her limp is quite pronounced. Can you see her running from the house, clouting Colonel Gauntlet over the head and then holding him down under the water with the rake for good measure?'

'No, I don't think you can fake her arthritic hands, and I suspect her hips are the same, or the knees.'

'Dobson?' asked Alasdair and then answered himself. 'He wants the job. Even though it is harder than he anticipated. If things go as I suspect and they all do go screaming for the hills, then he will be out of a job, presumably. I suppose it depends on how large the property Serena and Charles Gauntlet move to will be and whether they feel any loyalty to their old serv . . . domestic staff.'

'Now, Raoul Dufour. Tell me all about him.'

'He came over originally in 1914 with a host of refugees. He and his brother were separated in Belgium, but he was sure that his brother had also escaped to England. He spent four years trying to trace him through various rescue organisations while he worked as a chef at a London hotel. It was fine at first, but then as the war began to bite attitudes started to change and his treatment began to decline. He was, I think, resented for being alive and safe, while "our boys" were fighting and dying. Despite this, he gave up his chance for a free safe passage home at the end of the war, as he still hadn't found his brother. However, he found out from relatives in Belgium that they had been informed his brother had enlisted and been killed. This confused him as he knew he had weak lungs. Then about a year ago Dufour was told by a charity that his brother had been evacuated to Somerset. He came down here and began investigating.'

'Gosh, wouldn't it be extraordinary if it was the charity that my cousin Emma was volunteering with?' Tears began to well in her eyes as she thought of her dead cousin. Murdered a scant year ago. All of the family were picking up the pieces, but the pain was still raw.

'Mellie . . .' Alasdair reached out and laid his hand on her knee. 'What can I say?'

'Nothing.'

Alasdair heard the sob in her voice. He reached up

and brushed away the tears from her cheek.

'I hadn't thought this through any more than Davinia. The deaths at Pennstone Manor are still so painful and new and this just brings it all back.'

There was a silence for a moment or two as Alasdair allowed her to regain her equilibrium. The fire crackled. He was grateful that it was efficient and kept the room warm. There was no sound of rain, and the wind seemed to have died down. He really did not want them to stay here for any longer than possible. This was not a happy house. In fact, it had a positively poisonous atmosphere. The house? Or the people in it? Years ago, he would have laughed at Melissa's empathic feelings about places or objects, but since he had been blind and learned to pay attention, there was something that played on the outer edges of his senses that gave him information. From where, he had no idea. He was not sure he even wanted to know but was grateful for it nonetheless.

'So,' Melissa said, her voice under control, 'having found out Colonel Gauntlet had passed Dufour's unfit brother as fit and he then died, do we think the chef was blackmailing him?'

'I think it was more that he felt he was owed compensation. We shall need to check the will tomorrow, but I doubt there was anything in it. He had asked for a high salary and got it. I suspect his compensation was that he had made savings. After all, what was there to spend it on out here?'

'You know, thinking about the Colonel … despite his jovial exterior on Friday evening – I assume for our benefit – he was not a very pleasant man.'

'That, my dear, is an understatement.'

FORTY-SIX

Alasdair looked at her shrewdly. By now he knew totally instinctively exactly where she was in a room. 'I know you try and find the good in everyone, but he really was rotten. To try and manipulate his family from beyond the grave. To sit there on high, knowing he was responsible for sending local unfit men to the front. I suspect he was a bully and an arch manipulator, craving control and power and turning black and corrupt inside. At least with Roderick Gauntlet, what you see is what you get.'

'How could two cousins be so absolutely ghastly?' Melissa said. 'Oh but don't distract me. I'd like to go through my list in order. Another brandy? Thomas did bring the bottle, you know.'

Alasdair flipped up the glass on his Braille watch. 'All right.' He grinned. 'I forgot we came up early. It is only ten o'clock.'

'More coal on the fire?'

'I think it's warm enough. How much is there? Those will be the next things that run out if this household has not prepared for winter: coal, petrol, lamp oil and food.'

'How dire. We must get on and solve this. Oh, but then what do we do if we solve it and are still trapped here?'

'Now who's jumping ahead? Put Dufour as a possible but I suspect he will have a long enough alibi in the kitchens when we check tomorrow.'

'We now come to Hazel Richards, the governess. There was something you wanted to tell me about her, wasn't there?'

Alasdair proceeded to fill Melissa in on the conversation he had heard out in the hallway after the lights had gone out.

'You think she may be South African?'

'There is a connection certainly. She knew just the word to use and he certainly seemed to get the wind up. I wonder if he has been the source of her inappropriate riches you were telling me about. Costly perfume, expensive clothes.'

'No. I think not,' Melissa contradicted him. 'They would need trips to London or perhaps Bristol to buy. No, I think it is more likely that she comes from wealth. Either wealth lost – and given Roderick's track record that seems likely – or she still has the money and is here under false pretences for some sort of revenge.'

'You think she could have murdered the wrong person? That the intended victim was Roderick and Colonel Gauntlet got coshed instead?'

'I do wish you wouldn't use that word. It is so flippant. Bad 'un or not, it was still murder.'

'Yes, if she intended to murder him, then there can be no defence of justifiable homicide, as our American friends might call it.'

'But how could we prove it?' Melissa argued. 'And surely she has an alibi. She was in the schoolroom with the children. On the second floor. If she had left the children, she still would have had to run down two flights, either through the house and out of the front door, or down the servants' stairs and out through their quarters.'

'She could have come down the servants' stairs and out and back through the front door. We need to check where they come out on the ground floor.'

'It would still be a massive risk,' Melissa scoffed. 'There are far more Gauntlets and guests than there are servants. However, tomorrow I'll have a go at it. In fact, I could re-enact it from various points and then you could time it. If we did it at about the same time, we could see who notices us!'

'Great idea.' Alasdair tried to keep the indulgence out of his voice; she really was fun and sometimes, just sometimes, her ideas worked. 'How about Charles Gauntlet?'

'The psychology is all wrong.' Melissa was into her rhythm now. 'He couldn't stand up to his father. He allowed himself to be moulded into a character his father wanted but clearly was not him. Would he really have the strength of character to murder someone?'

'That is an odd way of putting it. He might have felt cornered, like a rat with no way out. They turn, don't they?'

'Yes, but a Jack Russell terrier always gets their rat. However, equating the Colonel with a Jack Russell is doing the breed a disservice, I think. I really can't see him as a murderer. His behaviour afterwards seems to me to show that his father's murder has given him permission to be himself. To do what he and Serena want. I suspect that if it hadn't happened, they would still be here until he died at ninety odd – of old age.'

'That is rather inspired, my dear. Keep up the reading of psychology – I now officially approve. And his wife?'

'Well, she has been allowed to develop an inferiority complex. Notice the affected accent and the desire to please the in-laws at all costs.' Melissa adopted a sonorous voice, making Alasdair chuckle. He rather thought the large brandies were beginning to have an effect on her. He only hoped she could read her notes tomorrow.

'But,' Melissa continued more sensibly, 'for her children she would do anything. If Colonel Gauntlet threatened them in any way then I would say look out. But I suspect she would just pack the children up and leave. She has wealthy parents, after all, so there is no motive to kill.'

Sheba whined from her bed in the corner.

'Golly, Alasdair, we forgot to let Sheba out for her run. I thought something was nagging me when I mentioned the Jack Russell.'

'Oh blast, I have taken my shoes off too.'

'I can go, she'll come with me,' Melissa ventured.

'No fear. Allow you two out alone? No telling what you would get up to. Come on. And bring the torch.'

FORTY-SEVEN

No lights shone under any of the doors and there were no lights over the stairs in the hallway or the entrance porch. Melissa began to lead the way, shining her torch here and there, but for the last set of stairs, Sheba and Alasdair took over. Melissa was stunned until she remembered that Alasdair would have counted the number of steps. She watched him step confidently onto the hall floor while she picked her way down, tentatively clinging to the bannister. 'Show off,' she muttered, and was rewarded with a chuckle.

'Don't distract me. I need to concentrate otherwise it tends to hurt.'

Remembering the bruises on his shins, she kept quiet. The front door was bolted. She pulled back the bolt and opened the door. It was cold, but the sky was clear and there was a winking of stars.

'That smell,' Alasdair said. 'Unique, or certainly new to me.'

'Do you think it means the waters are receding?'

'What are you asking me for?' he teased and pulled her close. 'Hurry up, Sheba, it is freezing,' he muttered.

Thankfully she was quick, and Melissa closed the door. The whole house seemed steeped in silence; the noise of the bolt being shunted seemed to echo around the great hall. They paused a moment but no one came running.

'If Thomas has got the electrical system to work, how long before it will kick in?'

'I have no idea, overnight at a guess. Come on, Melissa, a warm room awaits.'

He led the way. Sheba, off the lead, was more animated, and Melissa had to go slowly. The fear of falling was a strong deterrent. How brave Alasdair was, she suddenly thought. How would I cope if I was engulfed in permanent darkness and knew it was forever?

They reached their room without incident and, giggling, poured more brandy.

'Come on, let us get this finished,' Alasdair said. 'No. No, not the brandy. Our deliberations. We need to sleep. And have a glass of water.'

'Right, much as I hate to broach it, let us talk about Davinia. She is definitely strong enough in temperament. I can see her taking fast action, but why invite us down to solve her grandmother's supposed murder if she was going to commit one of her own?'

'It could be double bluff, but no, I think Davinia is quite safe from accusation. Now, Sheridan Kennard, what do you think?'

Melissa was flushed with pleasure from his genuinely consulting her and valuing her opinion. But she realised she was also flushed from the brandy. Her cheeks were hot and she put the glass down. Getting squiffy would never do. This was serious work. 'Assuming he is who he says he is, we will have to take him on trust. But can we?'

'I think we can take it as read as to who he is. Quite who he is working for and how it helps being in England is a bit of a stretch. Why not pursue Bernard Lyons in

America?'

'Perhaps they would rather not sully the markets over there by openly going after him?'

'But, Mellie, what Lyons is doing is not strictly illegal. Immoral, yes, but if people are prepared to risk a blind investment for high profits, then they must expect to get burned occasionally. And professional investors would factor losses into their investment portfolio. The problem here is that Roderick, allegedly using Bernard Lyons' scheme, is fleecing family.'

'So, no motive for Sheridan Kennard.'

'Well, as he is now engaged to Davinia, and presumably had that outcome in his mind, the money could be a motive, and he is certainly going over the finances with a fine-tooth comb. But to murder? No, I can't see it.' Alasdair shook his head.

'The Searles?'

'No, not unless they are barking.'

'I know it is a long shot, but I have to include her for consistency. Marjorie Gauntlet? I would not have thought she had the temperament for it.'

'Well, Mellie, some of these old fusspots are stronger than they seem. But no, you are right. I think we can discount her. But what are your feelings about the last of the Gauntlets – Petunia?'

'She certainly has the temperament. Sharp as a knife. But would she have the strength to whack him and hold him down? I am trying to remember. Was she walking with a stick on Friday evening? She certainly is today. I mean she is well into her eighties.'

'Yes. Sadly, I have to agree with your reasoning. Much as I would like to pin something on the old bat, I cannot see quite how she did it.'

'Then, Alasdair, we are left with Roderick, aren't we?'

'We are. Come on, let's get ready for bed, and if you can think of a way that we can trap him into confessing, let me know.'

FORTY-EIGHT

Melissa was yawning heavily when she finally came to bed. Alasdair could not fathom quite what it was that took up so much of her time before bed. The considering of the candidates for murder seemed to have conversely woken him up. He lay there long after Melissa had extinguished the lamp, listening to the hiss and pop of the fire, the odd creakings that could be expected in an old house like this and the pattering that, in a house with so little servants, could also be anticipated. He just hoped a mouse did not venture in here as it would be sure to antagonise Sheba, and then their sleep would be disturbed. Ha, what sleep? he thought. How on earth were they going to run Roderick Gauntlet to ground? He was a slippery character and would not be easy to catch. It certainly would not be in his character to readily confess. It would need painstaking police work, he suspected. There must be a trail from South Africa. Perhaps at the least they could charge him with fraud. But then would the family really want the publicity? Probably not, and then Roderick would get away with all his crimes. He suspected they were many.

If only the phone could be made to work, they could then set the police wheels in motion. Sheridan could also contact his agency. Between them, they must be able to find something to pin on him. Alasdair rolled over. If Roderick was the murderer, he had been clever with the rake and fork. Or very, very stupid. He slept.

***

He woke abruptly from a nightmare of the shell hole. His heart pounding, he wiped the sheen of sweat from his face and neck on the sheet. Melissa, beside him, groaned in her sleep but did not wake. He eased himself out of bed carefully. The room was cold now. He reached for his watch on the nightstand, lifting the glass and feeling for the time. It was five o'clock. So he had, after all, slept well. He was alert, as though something as well as the dream had roused him from sleep. But what could it be at this time in the morning? The servants stirring? He returned to bed and tried to force himself back to sleep. It had been a skill from the trenches, the ability to sleep anywhere at any time. Even through the pounding of the guns. The guns. Why had he been disturbed by a dream accompanied by guns? His eyelids became heavy and he slept again. What seemed like only moments later, he was awoken again – this time by the pounding on the bedroom door. It opened and he heard voice of Thomas; his valet's tone had him sitting up fully awake and alert.

'Sir, you and madam must get up. I have brought up some coffee. You are going to need it.'

'Why, what is it?' Alasdair asked. His heart had not yet returned to normal and he took some deep breaths, preparing for bad news. He shook Melissa awake.

'Roderick Gauntlet. He is dead. Shot. I have insisted that the door to his bedroom is locked and nothing is disturbed. But I think it needs someone with more authority to control the household.'

'Thank you, Thomas. You stand outside his room and make sure it is protected as much as possible. We will be up as soon as we are dressed.'

Melissa had already leapt out of bed, and she pressed a cup of coffee into his hand. 'Don't worry, it is not too hot. Drink it up. Shall I lay out your things on the bed?'

'Yes, anything. We need to get up there before anyone tampers too much with the evidence.'

This time, he ordered the ever-keen Sheba to stay and left her on her blanket. Melissa sped up the stairs with Alasdair's arm firmly tucked under hers, his other hand firm on the bannister. They turned left once they reached the second-floor landing. Outside Roderick's room stood Thomas, Charles Gauntlet and Sheridan Kennard.

'Thank goodness you are here at last. Your man is refusing to open the door.' Charles sounded furious.

'Whatever happens now, the police will have to be involved, and this will be treated as a crime scene. Even if it is an accident. The less people who have access and leave fingerprints about the place, the less problems the police will have solving the issue. And the less likely anyone innocent will be mixed up in it.'

'Oh God, I never thought of that. But it is suicide, isn't it? Sheridan, you tell him.'

'How are we going to play this?' Sheridan said. 'Say, Charles, why don't you go downstairs, get the staff to serve breakfast as normal and keep everyone calm? Especially as you are head of the household. You need to take charge.'

Melissa grinned at Sheridan as Charles left. 'That

was a neat piece of psychology.'

'Yes, well done,' Alasdair said. 'Right, fill me in on what has happened, please, Sheridan.'

'You include your wife still? It is not a pretty sight in there. He is shot through the head.'

Melissa grimaced but said, 'No, I will be fine. I am his eyes and I am not a stranger to murder,' she added, crossing her fingers behind her back.

Alasdair caught her hands in the movement and whispered in her ear, 'You will be fine. You are a brave woman. I know it.'

Melissa straightened her spine, drew back her shoulders and said, 'Well, talk us through it first. Who found the body?'

'His mother apparently. She picked up the gun and threw it across the room, either in fury or who knows what reaction to seeing her son dead. Her shriek alerted the governess, Miss Richards. She rushed downstairs and woke Davinia. Miss Richards has taken the children to their parents' room for now. I have sent her to get dressed and asked her to go downstairs to the dining room, but first to send up Nurse Foote. That means the other half of this floor is now empty.

'Let me see, Nurse Foote took one look and declared the corpse extinct of life. I can confirm it is Roderick Gauntlet who is dead. Nurse Foote is tending to Petunia Gauntlet, his mother, as we speak. Petunia is not in a good way. Neither is Dunmore. He still hasn't regained consciousness and is turning a nasty colour, which could mean his organs are failing. Apparently he needs a hospital.'

'Phew.' Alasdair whistled. 'I am seriously impressed,

man. That is a great summary. Well, was it suicide?'

'Can we go back in? Thomas is mighty ferocious.' Sheridan chuckled.

'Yes. Thomas, you go in with them. Touch as little as possible.'

Melissa watched with trepidation as the door opened, hoping she was not going to disgrace herself. After all, she was with two battle-hardened veterans of the World War. When she looked, she found it was the smell that was the worst. The blood did not concern her. She had spent many weeks at her grandfather's estate where they seemed to hunt anything that moved. 'Isn't it a rather odd way of killing yourself? He has been shot through the forehead. I mean, he must have held the gun at arm's reach in front of him. What if his arms shook? He would have missed or just maimed himself. Wouldn't it be more natural to put the gun to the side of the head?'

'You're damned right, of course.' Sheridan sighed. 'I had been hoping this was a nice neat suicide. Remorse from killing his cousin Colonel Gauntlet and very possibly the murder of Frank Dunmore, if he dies. That would tie it up and release the family. It would not be pleasant but they would bear it.'

'Is there a suicide note?' called Alasdair from the threshold. 'I'll stay here. No point me blundering all over the place.'

'I cannot see any note,' Melissa said. 'Can either of you see anything?' she asked Thomas and Sheridan.

'He was very drunk last night,' Alasdair said. 'He might have been so incapable that he was unable to write one. Or his mind really was unbalanced.'

'But if that was the case, wouldn't his arms and

hands be shaking? It would make shooting himself very, excuse the pun, hit and miss.' Melissa wasn't convinced suicide was that simple an explanation.

'He might have wanted to stare death down the barrel of a gun and got lucky?' Thomas tried. Melissa looked at him. Was he too trying to find the easy way out?

'That may be what happened, but where is the proof? No suicide note. An odd way to kill yourself. The gun not in his hand and we cannot say we have proof that he killed his cousin, if that is being thought of as a motive for suicide. It could just as easily be murder. Why on earth did Petunia Gauntlet move the gun? It has ruined any hope of gaining a simple solution.'

'Yeah, I was kinda hoping you'd take the easy story,' Sheridan said. 'But I have to agree. If I was not about to join this family and investigating at home, then this would be a helluva fishy crime scene.'

FORTY-NINE

'Right.' Alasdair thumped the door post with the side of his fist. 'I think we need to work together. Sheridan, you have to realise that what you say or think may be tinged with bias. I don't know you well enough, obviously, to know whether you are the sort of investigator who pursues the truth at all costs. I am more practical, but I do not want to let a murderer off scot-free. Your fiancée believes her grandmother was the first victim, which points to someone bumping the family off rather systematically. If that is true and it was not Roderick Gauntlet, then you may inherit a problem, Sheridan.'

'I agree. Why on earth won't that danged water go away?'

Melissa was looking with disgust at the body in the sturdy wing-backed chair. It had taken most of the impact of the body falling back and the blood splatter. The chair must have rocked back but then righted itself, sending the head onto the chest. She tried to ignore the gaping hole and what must be brains. 'Does someone own a camera in the house? One we can use to take photos of the body and this room? At some point we are going to have to remove the body. It will start to stink.'

'Ever practical, my darling.' Alasdair's voice was laced with approval.

'Yeah, one great dame.' Melissa gave Sheridan what could only be described as a look. He cleared his throat and continued, 'I have a camera. Thomas, can you use one? I would prefer if someone else took the pictures. No one connected to the family in any way.'

'Very sensible.' Alasdair sounded as if he was attempting to stifle laughter. When Melissa looked up, she saw Thomas grinning, and then wondered what she had missed. She looked at Sheridan, who shrugged.

'I rather think Mr Charters and myself were rather nonplussed that the Honourable Melissa Charters, granddaughter of a baron, should be called "a great dame"!' Thomas explained.

Melissa howled with laughter suddenly and they all joined in. 'I hope it was a compliment,' she said primly.

'The greatest of compliments,' Sheridan solemnly assured her.

She laughed again and then, catching sight of the body, realised it could quickly be turning into hysteria. Her laugh ended on a little sob. 'Do you know what I think? I could do with a brandy. Brandy with breakfast. Best cure for murder.'

'Sheridan, do we know the time of the murder?' Alasdair asked. 'I was awoken at five this morning but it could have been just dream. We are on the far side of the house, after all. Who else may have heard the shot?'

Thomas walked across to the corpse, opened the jacket and felt inside. 'The body is cold, so he has been dead for some time. We need to check with the nurse about time of death. The maids may have heard. They are above, and the obvious is Petunia, immediately below, as is Mrs Marjorie Gauntlet. If you think you heard something, then Miss Gauntlet and Mr and Mrs Charles Gauntlet should have heard something.'

'Well I for one heard nothing,' Sheridan said. 'But then I am a really sound sleeper. We need to question everyone downstairs.'

'Rigor mortis has not set in, sir,' Thomas added. 'So it is eight o'clock now. If the shot was fired at about five a.m., that would tally with your timing.'

'Thomas, you have been studying!' Melissa exclaimed. 'Clever you.'

'That would sort of agree with what I would presume,' Sheridan added. 'Good call, Thomas.'

'We will need confirmation from Nurse Foote,' Alasdair said. 'But good show, Thomas. Can you see if there was anything lying around that could have muzzled the gun? You know, silenced it a bit? If I heard the shot, and it is a big if, then why didn't all the people you have mentioned, Sheridan, raise the alarm at five o'clock?'

'Not a clue. That's why we need information,' Sheridan replied.

'Have you found the gun?' Melissa asked.

'I didn't look. Didn't want to scrabble around and disturb the scene.'

'Did you talk to Petunia? Did she give any idea where she threw it? Of course, her fingerprints will be all over the gun, so that won't help the police. What was the gun?' Alasdair asked.

'A service revolver,' Thomas said. He indicated its current resting place to Melissa and Sheridan. 'It is in the right-hand corner of the room. Unfortunately, sir, this room is a total mess. It looks like it has not been cleaned recently and is untidy and slovenly. Dirty clothes all over the place, glasses, plates.'

'OK, I get the general idea. Thank you, Thomas,' Alasdair acknowledged. 'I agree with Sheridan – we should leave it all as undisturbed as possible for the police when they can get here. If the noise of the shot presents a problem, I suggest we might search later. Sheridan, can you go and get your camera now? The people downstairs won't be going anywhere. They can wait.'

He hoped that he sounded confident but he was seriously rattled. Crime scenes were not the place for a blind man. For a start, the smell was almost overwhelming and made him want to gag. Was it the same for the others? Or was it his heightened senses that made it so damn awful? He was seriously impressed with Thomas. Had he anticipated that this sort of situation might arise? But how? Then it came to him. Melissa. She was far too astute not to realise that there would be some situations in which male help would be needed. He was frankly amazed that she had stuck it out in that room for so long. As if in answer to his thoughts, she grasped his arm as she walked past him into the hallway. Still holding onto him, she stepped back against the wall and slumped.

'Well, that was absolutely appalling. When Meg died at Pennstone at least I could run away and leave it to the police,' she gasped. 'Thomas, come on out now. For heaven's sake. Gosh, you were absolutely ripping. Aren't we lucky that he has a calm head when faced with a dead body, and a horrid one at that?'

'Sadly, madam, I saw quite a few dead bodies in the war. Most of them worse than this. Shrapnel and shells an absolute bugger for a body to contend with. Pardon my French, madam.'

'No, you swear away, Thomas. Don't mind me, absolutely. I could do with a bit of that myself. Alasdair, you will have to teach me to swear.'

Unfortunately, Alasdair knew she was absolutely serious.

FIFTY

Sheridan Kennard came puffing down the landing at that point. He had clearly run all the way and back. He had his camera with him. Melissa noticed, with interest, it was a Kodak, but before she could ask all the questions she wanted, Alasdair was pulling her away.

'Thomas, can you stay here and then lock the room?' He added quietly, 'Quick, Melissa, take me next door. We must talk to Nurse Foote and Petunia.'

Melissa led him back along the landing and paused before Petunia's bedroom door.

'No, don't knock,' he hissed. 'Let's take them by surprise.'

Melissa opened the door and they stepped in. Nurse Foote turned around, and Melissa was surprised to see something furtive fleeting over her face. She tried to hide it, but Melissa could see that this was a woman who seldom dissembled and was not practised in it.

'What is the matter?' Melissa asked, her voice deliberately bland.

'She has had a seizure or it could be apoplexy. Either are serious, especially at her age. She keeps trying to say something but I can't quite catch it. Her speech is very slurred and she is in and out of consciousness. I am not sure you could rely on what she is saying.'

Petunia was lying propped up on a number of pillows. Melissa could see that one side of her face had dropped. She now appeared tiny and vulnerable. The spirited irascible old woman was no more. Just a small husk of an elderly woman. She did indeed seem to be mumbling.

'She keeps asking for you.' She pointed at Alasdair.

'You.' Melissa nudged him

'Me?' Alasdair exclaimed. 'What has she been saying?' His voice was tempered with suspicion.

'Oh, nothing I can tell you. It would not be fair. I mean, I do not have her permission. To divulge what she is saying. While ill.' Nurse Foote was twittering like a small bird.

'If it has a bearing on the murders here, then it is vitally important for the family,' Melissa urged.

'The family. What do they understand about ordinary people? Living in their huge house high on the hill.' She sounded bitter. 'I have no need to help them.'

'But the children,' Melissa persisted. 'Little Lucy and Robert. Should they grow up with the stain of murder?' She pressed on. 'We are not the police. We are not family. You can trust us.'

'But can I?' Nurse Foote laughed coldly. 'Listen to you, your accent. You toffs all stay together. What would you know about working class families?' She paused. 'But, he, Alasdair, he has tasted suffering, and plenty of it I'd say. Bring him up a chair and leave us.' Then, seeing the look on Melissa's face, she added, 'Don't be a fool, girl. I'm a nurse, I preserve life. I'll bring him back safe to you. Just look in on Dunmore, would you? I'm worried about him.'

Melissa took Alasdair's hand in hers. 'Are you all right?'

Alasdair squeezed it back. 'Yes, I will be fine. Also check if the electricity is working. Take Thomas with you.'

Melissa realised that in his turn he was warning her to be safe. She left the room, just in time to see Thomas locking Roderick Gauntlet's room. 'Come on, Thomas, we need to check on Dunmore for Nurse Foote. Petunia Gauntlet is in a bad way. Alasdair is staying as she is apparently muttering about the murders.'

'You are calling them murders then, madam?' Thomas sounded eager.

'Well, wasn't it an odd way to kill himself? Bullet to the temple would be more certain, don't you think?'

'No telling, really, he was that drunk last night. Should be up to a coroner by all rights, but fat chance of that any time soon. And we'll have to remove that body. The room is warm. The fire only just going out. He'll start to stink soon and no mistake. Madam,' he added.

Melissa's stomach gave a little flip of complaint, and she shivered. 'Come on, let's check on Dunmore and then on the electricity as Alasdair suggests.'

They went to Colonel Gauntlet's old room where Dunmore was temporarily residing. His breathing was very shallow, and he seemed to be turning a strange colour, almost yellow. Clearly he was now seriously ill. He would not be able to help with anything about the estate any time soon.

'Jaundice, seen it before, madam. He's a goner. This is some benighted house. The sooner we're out of it, the better.'

'I suspect that as soon as the flood recedes, they will all be going. You are right. I don't like it here.'

'The levels are all right, and Somerset folk are the bee's knees. You've just caught it at a bad time.'

'Do you know it then?' Melissa was surprised Thomas had not mentioned it.

'No, but we spent some time with the Somerset Light Infantry. Great bunch of lads and they told me all about home. Always wanted to come, but not like this.'

'Come on, we need to send someone up to sit with him. We cannot leave him alone. It would be just too awful.' She looked around the room; it was magnificently furnished in rich red tones that the Colonel seemed to have replicated all over the house. Dunmore looked as frail as the patient upstairs, lying in a huge four-poster bed with heavy damask coverings, like some fading king. At least it should be comfortable, she thought irrelevantly. Her brain seemed to be all over the place. She needed to pull herself together. They were not out of danger yet. 'Come on, Thomas. We need to stop at the dining room. Someone must sit with him.'

Uncharacteristically, Thomas stilled her arm as she reached for the door handle. 'I am going to look at the electrics. You stay with the family. Do not go off on your own or Major Charters will have my guts for garters. Please, madam.'

She nodded and opened the door.

FIFTY-ONE

The atmosphere was tense when Melissa entered and became the attention of all eyes in the room. Everyone seemed to be there, including the children and Hazel Richards.

'Someone needs to sit with Dunmore. He has taken a turn for the worse. He should not be alone. Nurse Foote is with Petunia. She too is very ill. Nurse Foote is staying with her.'

Davinia stood and took over. 'Miss Richards, would you please go and sit with Dunmore? He is in Father's room, if you didn't know. Serena, you can cope with the children for now, can't you?'

'Of course, Davinia. It will be fun for them to have a break from the schoolroom.' Serena's voice was light, no doubt to reassure the children, but her eyes were panicked.

'Where is Alasdair?' Davinia asked. 'And, for that matter, Sheridan?'

'Alasdair is staying with Nurse Foote and Aunt Petunia.' Anticipating Davinia's interruption, Melissa said, 'He will be fine up there out of the way for the moment. Thomas can take them up some breakfast.' She mentally crossed her fingers. She sincerely hoped Alasdair would be safe, and she knew he would hate that she implied his blindness was a weakness. However, those around the table were all to ready to accept her excuse and let it go. 'Thomas is checking on the electrics. Would the lights just come on automatically if the batteries were working?'

'I am sorry, I haven't got a clue.' Charles's frustration showed in his voice. 'This is very bad news about Dunmore. He was such a use— valued member of staff. We would be lost without him. I think I had better go and join Thomas and see if he can show me what is what, assuming he has got it working. The boilers will need attending to.'

Melissa raised her eyebrows. She had no concerns for Thomas even if Charles should be a murderer. He was no match for Thomas's wiry strength. He really was a gem. She wondered if Charles Gauntlet had ever considered his domestic staff.

'But where is Sheridan?' Davinia's voice rose.

'Thomas took some photographs of Roderick's room with Sheridan's camera. Can Sheridan develop them here?'

'I don't think so. But why?'

Melissa sauntered over to her and whispered in her ear, 'For the coroner. We are going to have to move your uncle's body if the police can't get here soon. If you catch my drift.'

It appeared Davinia did, as she went a little pale. Melissa carried on around the table to the sideboard and chaffing dishes. Despite everything, she was now starving. There still seemed to be plenty of breakfast food; no kidneys but perhaps that was just as well. The thought of them suddenly made her a little queasy. But she forced herself to put bacon, a sausage and scrambled eggs on her plate. It all smelt spiffing. Sitting at a vacant place, she looked up and saw that everyone was looking at her expectantly. Just how much should she tell them? She popped a forkful of scrambled egg in her mouth because she was starving and she needed time to consider her answers.

'Well, as you may have gathered, Roderick Gauntlet is dead. He has been shot. It is unclear as to whether it is suicide or murder,' she decided on.

'Children, have you finished?' Serena stood up. 'We will be in the drawing room. Little ears, you know.'

'Well, keep together,' Melissa said. She didn't want to frighten them but this was a pretty desperate situation. She looked around the table: Marjorie, Davinia and the Searles. As long as they didn't go off, they should all be safe.

'But surely it makes sense that he killed Father and then has committed suicide,' Davinia said. The door opened and Sheridan came in. 'Please tell her, Sheridan.'

'What am I meant to tell her, honey?' he said as he made a beeline for the breakfast.

'That Uncle Roddy killed Father and has now committed suicide. It all fits.'

'It may fit and very neatly.' He glanced at Melissa, no doubt wondering what she had said. 'But we need to be sure.'

'Really?'

Sheridan walked over to Davinia and put his arms around her: a flagrant display of affection of which Melissa approved.

'Listen, honey. This has to be thought out. We need to have covered every angle to satisfy the police. I don't know what the cops are like here but at home they are regular hounds.'

'But our local constable will be no problem,' Davinia began.

'But it won't be him. He will have to call in his superiors. They will send an inspector at least. They probably will involve the chief constable as well and he may call in Scotland Yard.'

'Scotland Yard?' Davinia sounded appalled.

'Honey, there have been two deaths here. Three if Dunmore dies. Four if your aunt goes as well. They cannot ignore it or just hush it up.'

'And you don't want that either,' Melissa said. 'All those rumours and pointing fingers. We must try and sort it out ourselves and then give a credible story to the police and the coroner that will satisfy them.'

Charles coming in, followed by Thomas and Dobson, disrupted her thread of thought.

'Excuse me,' said Dobson. 'I turned off the switches last night when the lights failed. You just switch them on here, like this.'

Melissa almost clapped with joy as one of the standard lamps lit up.

FIFTY-TWO

Dobson turned the other switch and that standard lamp too came on.

'Mr Gauntlet, do you think you might have the hang of it?' Thomas asked. The important thing is to keep the motor topped up with petrol. Much easier than trying to start the whole thing up again. It really is like a car engine. You might need a mechanic to show you how to grease it and deal with any problems. How is Dunmore, madam, if I might ask?' he enquired, turning to Melissa.

'Not well, Thomas. Nurse Foote now thinks he is dying.' Melissa had started on toast. 'Golly, I just remembered. Can you arrange some breakfast to go up to Alasdair and Nurse Foote?'

Thomas glanced at Dobson and, getting the assenting nod, made a quick exit.

Marjorie gave a deep groan and clutched her face with her hands.

'Are you all right, Mother? Not feeling unwell again?' Davinia was all concern.

'No, dear, but all this death, how are we going to cope?' she wailed.

'Now come on, Marjorie,' Arthur Searle cajoled her. 'Buck up. We faced worse situations than this in India. Someone was always dying.'

'Oh, yes, yes, you are right. But that is why we came back to England and now look what has happened.' Her voice rose, tinged with hysteria.

'For goodness sake, Mother.' Charles's voice was firm. This was a very different man from the one they had encountered on Friday night. 'Do pack it in. Set an example. I don't want the children upset any more than is necessary. Hopefully they are too young to understand what is going on. But, Davinia, you also must see that if this situation is not sorted out, we will all be ruined, including the children. You may want to go to America, and good luck to you, but the rest of us like it here and want to remain in the area. If this is not solved, no one will receive us. You must see, if we have nothing to hide then we must help Melissa, Alasdair and Sheridan as much as we can.' He raised his eyebrows at his sister.

'Well, I certainly have nothing to hide. Does anyone else in this room?'

They all looked around at each other, shaking their heads.

'Well, that is all well and good,' Melissa said. 'I say, Sheridan, could I borrow you? Perhaps we could go into the study? Alasdair and I had some ideas last night.'

'Well, I must go and soothe the chef. I presume, Charles, you are happy with me continuing in my role of chatelaine pro tem?' Davinia wasn't even trying to sound arch, thought Melissa. Would peace and light now arise in this house? Not if there was still a murderer stalking the residents there wouldn't be.

She really wanted to try to help these people, heaven only knows why. Or was it, she thought shrewdly, more that she wanted to satisfy herself? Either way, there was work to be done. Sheridan was standing by the door and he opened it for her. She led the way to the study. She settled at the desk and Sheridan sat before her.

'Well, Melissa, fire away.'

'So, are you completely au fait with the will now? Assuming it is the right one.'

'Yeah, but didn't you make notes yesterday?'

'I only checked the major bequests, how it affected the family. I need to see if there were any smaller bequests for the servants and such like.'

'There was nothing for the maids. Perhaps he thought they would hop it if he left them anything. He left the Dobsons £100.'

'So they could retire if they wanted to? If they were careful?'

'You tell me. There is also an interesting bequest to Raoul Dufour – £50, provided his restaurant always has a curried dish on the menu. Some kinda joke?'

'Perhaps a warped one. Although I think Dufour will be pleased. He does want to open a restaurant.' Melissa told him all about Dufour and his brother.

'That Colonel Gauntlet was a right bastard underneath all that bluster, wasn't he? I wonder how he lived with himself. And how many other stories there are.'

'I think neither of the cousins were very palatable,' Melissa said. 'I wonder if Roderick Gauntlet left a will?'

'I don't think he was killed for his money, do you?'

'But we need to find out what he has done with it all,' Melissa persisted.

'Well, I am none too keen to face that room again I can tell ya.'

'At some point we will have to move the body. Thomas estimates we have about a day,' she muttered.

'Look, from here we look over where the moat was. Can you see it from here?'

Sheridan stood up. 'No, there're bushes in the way.'

Melissa joined him. 'Yes, you are right. They go all the way along. OK, you go out the front door and make your way to where the body was found and wave.'

'Ah I see what you're doing. Just hang on and I'll do it.'

Melissa went to the window and stood watching. There was a clear path from the front door to the little bridge. She saw Sheridan almost immediately. If she could see him from the ground floor, then anyone looking out of an upper window in this direction could have seen the murderer. She came out of the study and went to the open front door and called, 'Just stand in the middle of the drive just below the bridge, will you?'

He stood there. She could see him easily. It was quite clear that anyone approaching the position of the Colonel from that direction could be seen. Therefore, they, for example, would have been visible when they came round from the back of the house that way.

Sheridan was waving at her. 'Come and look at this,' he called.

Nervously, she ventured out onto the drive and walked towards him.

'Look,' he said, 'the water is going.'

He was right. There was more of the drive visible; it was clearing but there was a lot of debris left behind, branches and rocks. The bank below the moat could now be seen. The water in the ditch was moving, contained as it was between the banks. Presumably it was draining somewhere. She hoped it was not adding to any devastation below them. She said as much to Sheridan, who said it would be draining into the river and then out to sea.

'Even if it does drain, it will not be very safe to drive in or out until it is all cleared,' she said. 'Did anyone look to see if there was a boat? A canoe would be ideal.'

'Nope, not that I heard. Gee, so what have we learned? Just that the murderer could have been seen but it looks like no one saw him or her and they lucked out?'

They were walking back up the drive with Sheridan occasionally bending and lobbing debris into the shrubbery either side. Melissa was still ruminating over ways someone could have got to the murder scene unseen when Elsie appeared at the front door calling, 'Quick, quick, sir, madam! You are needed.'

FIFTY-THREE

They broke into a run and followed her into the house.

'Madam, you need to go up to Mrs Petunia Gauntlet's room. Your husband is calling for you.'

Melissa, with a quick smile at Elsie and a nod to Sheridan, hared up the stairs, only pausing for a moment outside Petunia's room to catch her breath. She opened the door and went in.

'Close the door behind you, Melissa, please. Bring out your notebook and begin taking notes. This is vital. Nurse Foote is refusing to be a witness against her patient.'

Melissa pulled up a chair, took her notebook out of the deep pocket of her cardigan and sat poised ready.

'Say that again, Petunia, slowly please.' Alasdair coaxed.

Petunia's voice was weak and slurred. One side of her face had dropped and she seemed to be having difficulty with her tongue. 'I killed my son,' she wheezed. There was silence, then she continued. 'Roderick.' Silence again. 'I shot him. With his own gun. I did nothing else.' She collapsed into the pillows.

Nurse Foote wiped Petunia's mouth with a handkerchief.

Alasdair said, 'Petunia, did you also kill your nephew, William Gauntlet?'

There was no reply. The woman seemed to have lost

consciousness.

'Enough,' snapped Nurse Foote. 'Don't harass a dying woman. She's confessed, isn't that enough for you?'

Melissa noted the time and who was present. 'The police will need this. I respect your view, Nurse Foote, but if she also killed William, then we have the solution and no one else should need suffer.'

Nurse Foote pursed her lips and gave a small movement with her shoulders, a little shake of her upper body. Melissa could see that she did not agree with Alasdair in some deep fundamental way. But why? Did she want the family to suffer? Was she protecting someone?

Alasdair tried again, raising his voice, enunciating the words clearly and carefully. 'Petunia. Did you kill your nephew, William?'

Still silence.

'Let me try.' Melissa knelt beside the bed and took Petunia's hand in hers; it was cold to the touch and faintly repellent, so small and bony, skeletal. 'Petunia,' she whispered, close to her ear, 'tell me, Melissa, did you kill William?' The hand twitched and it was all she could do not to seize her hand back. The fingers clutched Melissa's, surprisingly strong. Petunia's eyelids fluttered but did not open. She seemed to be making a massive effort.

'No.' It was spat out, spittle following and settling upon her face, then quieter, as if she was using the last of her strength, Petunia whispered, slurring, 'Not William.'

'Thank you, Petunia. You can rest now.' Melissa said

quietly with all the compassion she could muster. She made as if to pull her hand away, but there was what might have been a cackle from the bed and the fingers hung on to her. Petunia coughed and her breathing stopped, only to start a few seconds later with a deep drawing slow breath. Then silence. Then breath came again.

'The death rattle's started. Won't be long now. I must check on Dunmore and inform her family. They may want to say their goodbyes.' Nurse Foote's voice was tart. 'I'm sure you can cope now. You'll get nothing more from her. I hope you're satisfied.' As an admonition, it was devastating. She shut the door quietly behind her.

'Melissa,' Alasdair's voice croaked. His anguish evident.

Melissa knew he would find it hard to come to terms with later, but now was not the time. She picked up his hand as well with her free hand. Her comfort knew no bounds. She had sat with dying young men in the hospital she volunteered at during the war. She knew her role. 'Not now, let her die in peace. She has done a wonderful thing. A glorious thing, confessing. It is a true gift. She will be remembered with gratitude.'

She began a low litany of compassion and love, tears trickling down her cheeks, and when she looked at Alasdair, his face too was wet with tears. How many men had they both sat with like this during the war? Yet this was her first sitting in with a natural death of an elderly woman.

The door opened. Looking around, she saw Davinia slip in. She approached with a couple of cushions that she grabbed from a chair and positioned under Melissa's knees to relieve the pressure, for which Melissa was inordinately grateful. Davinia began to read from the Bible. 'Let not your heart be troubled; you believe in God, believe also in Me. In My Father's house are many mansions; if it were not so, I would have told you. I go to prepare a place for you.'

Davinia's deep voice flowed over the three listeners while she continued with the tried and well-known passages they had both been taught to use in the war to end all wars. Her voice, steady and strong, did not waver as the breathing of Petunia became slower and slower, extending until she breathed no more.

FIFTY-FOUR

Melissa gently extracted her fingers from those of Petunia and stood up, staggering a little. Her knees and back ached from the amount of time she had spent knelt on the floor.

Davinia came over and gave Melissa a hug. They stood swaying for a few minutes.

Alasdair was oblivious to all of this. He was back in a field hospital in France, lying on a low pallet. His head was bandaged and he had a hell of a headache. He was waiting for transport back to Blighty. Beside him was a priest reading the same passage he was hearing now. He could smell the tang of the hospital, a sweet rotting smell overlaid with disinfectant. The priest had a beautiful voice, deep and resonant, a gentle Scottish burr. He had been kind, but Alasdair had found it hard to be gracious, wrapped up tight in his misery. If he was permanently blind, how would he cope? How would his family – and Melissa? He would have to let her go. Get a divorce. That would be best. Set her free. She couldn't be saddled with him now. All these thoughts ran around his mind as tight as the bandage and twice as exhausting. The priest's voice was soothing, and he began to doze.

The doctor had just told him as gently as possible that it was highly unlikely that his sight would return. He had been found on the floor of the church. Again, why had the woman praying in the church not intervened or at least gone to fetch help? Maybe she had and then slipped away, unwilling to be caught up the in military machine. But she must have seen him being hit, or had it been her?

Alasdair opened his eyes, realising that he had drifted off. The old woman had stopped breathing. Melissa was no longer holding his hand. She was talking with Davinia.

What memory was he still chasing? Memories that he had forgotten? Or his mind had obliterated? Yes, the voice of a woman. A woman praying in a church in France, and then he had it. He knew where he had heard that voice before, not so long ago. Why had he had the memory now? Why not then, dammit? When he had the time and the opportunity to challenge her? Melissa was talking to him. He must pack these thoughts away. There would be time, plenty of time, for them to enter the light. He had time. He could be a patient man. He must search for the truth.

'Darling, are you all right?' Melissa took his face in her hands and kissed the top of his head. She was whispering.

'Yes, just a little groggy, another damn flashback.' What it cost his pride to say that. It had taken years for him to admit to her that he even had them. They were less now, but no less vivid.

'I must go and get Nurse Foote just to confirm Great Aunt Petunia has definitely passed away. Can you stay here for a little longer?' Davinia was blowing her nose.

Alasdair hoped that meant that at least one person in the household would be mourning Petunia. 'Melissa, can you make sure you have everything written down.

Including that "no" at the end. The police will want to have her deathbed confession.'

'We still have to find who killed William Gauntlet.'

'Yes, and quick. Damn, I should have asked Davinia to keep quiet about her confession. Was she here then?'

Melissa was quiet for a moment, clearly thinking, 'No, she came in afterwards. Of course, she could have been listening outside the door, but I doubt it.'

'Let us keep this confession under our hats for now then. Wait, Nurse Foote heard it. We must ask her to keep shtum. We need to keep the murderer complacent, and then we might catch them through an overconfident slip up.'

'I have just had a ghastly thought.' Melissa gasped. 'We have another body to dispose of. That outhouse is going to become a morgue.'

'Well we can't worry about that now.' He flipped up the glass of his Braille watch. 'You do realise it is lunch time.' And, as if in answer, a gong sounded from below.

'Gosh, yes, I am starving.' Melissa had forgotten to whisper and he felt her start beside him.

'Don't worry, she can't hear you now. Extreme emotion does make one hungry, you know, nothing to feel guilty about.'

'And the chef, Raoul Dufour, is such a good cook. You do realise that you did not ask her about her sister, Lavender?' Melissa added.

'She had been rambling about Lavender before you came in but nothing, I think, that could be useful. Although she was worried about something to do with her sister, but to be honest I forgot later. I felt such a cad questioning her anyway. Nurse Foote saw to that. I doubt I would have raised it even had I remembered it.'

'Oh, darling, you absolutely did the right thing. You have solved one murder and Lavender … well, she is dead and buried and we can just leave her to rest in peace.'

'But will she if she was murdered?' Doubt and depression had crept back into the edges of Alasdair's mind. 'We need to question the governess. Find out what she knew about Roderick Gauntlet. That may explain a few things, and I think after lunch we should search Petunia's rooms.'

'Righty ho. I will catch Dobson, or Thomas – he seems to be shaping up as an under-butler rather well, don't you think? We need this room and her sitting room locked.'

'Good idea, Mellie. You are really thinking like a detective. What about Sheridan? Shall we leave him out for the moment? I'd hate to put him in the position of keeping anything from the family.'

The door opened and closed; Alasdair heard Nurse Foote's steps approaching.

'So, she died, did she? That were quick. I suppose she didn't fight it. So many of them do, you know. Get what you wanted?' Her voice was shrewd. 'Hold on. Let me confirm life is extinct.' There were a few minutes' pause. 'So, yes, she's dead. The body will have to be moved at least by tomorrow. I'll douse this fire, that should help, and just open this window a chink. It's not as if there's anyone else alive on this wing to complain about a draught.' She gave a quick snort that could have been nearly amusement or it could have been derision. 'So what next, Mr Charters?'

Alasdair heard from the chill in her voice that he had still not been forgiven. It would be hard going if he had made an enemy of this efficient and caring woman. 'Please tell no one of what you heard and saw in this room. We still have one more murder to solve, as you now know. I would ask you to keep quiet. It is essential we do not alert the murderer. How is Dunmore?'

Nurse Foote gave a start that he heard from the soles of her shoes hitting the floor. 'What? Oh, Dunmore, sorry, I'm getting jumpy. Too many deaths, and this won't be the last. Even if we could get a doctor here now, I doubt Frank Dunmore'd survive.' She sounded bitter. 'It'll be a long slow death. He was a strong, fit man. I must return. He's my patient now. Ask them to send me a tray, would you? I want to spend as little time as possible with that family.'

FIFTY-FIVE

'She really doesn't like them, does she?' Melissa commented as Nurse Foote left. 'Come on, I'll take you outside and go and fetch Thomas.' However, when she opened the door, Thomas was standing there waiting. 'Spiffing, Thomas, just who we wanted to see. Can you find the keys to this room and her sitting room and lock them?'

'I will fetch them immediately. I came to tell you luncheon is ready.' The gong sounded from below.

'Can you arrange a tray for Nurse Foote? She will be staying with Dunmore.'

Thomas nodded and departed swiftly. Melissa rather thought he might be on serving duty at luncheon once again.

They slipped into their room and fetched Sheba. She would need to be let out before lunch; they had been rather longer than anticipated. Rushing round Alasdair, she wagged her tail excitedly and was rewarded with a thorough fuss being made of her. They let her out of the front door. It was getting colder. The sky was clear, no sign of further rain.

'After lunch let's take her for a long walk. It may be cold, but I think we need some fresh air after that morning, don't you?'

'Well you know, Alasdair, much as I would love to spend the afternoon in front of a roaring fire, I think you are right. We can also talk things over. The water is definitely beginning to recede. Sheridan and I were able to walk quite a lot further down the drive. He thinks somewhere there must be someone pumping the water into the rivers.'

'Yes, someone might have a steam pump, and if the rivers have subsided somewhat there would be room for the excess water to be carried away.'

'Great, here is Sheba back. Come on, I want to see what the chef has rustled up this time.'

He did them proud. Fresh crusty rolls and a thick vegetable soup. Salmon fishcakes. Melissa assumed the salmon must have been tinned, but he had added some interesting herbs that she had not tried before. She rather thought she might like French cooking. They certainly were superior to any fishcakes she had eaten before. For dessert there was an apple tart with custard.

Everyone around the table was very subdued, which was perhaps appropriate considering the third death in the family had occurred shortly before lunch. The children, and presumably Hazel Richards, were having lunch back up in the nursery, but Serena Gauntlet confirmed she would be playing with the children after lunch. So that meant that she and Alasdair would have time to question the governess. Perhaps after they had searched Petunia's rooms.

Sheridan and Charles were planning an expedition down the drive and attempting to make some sort of decision about breaking out of the confines of the property.

Davinia was talking to her mother about housekeeping. Apparently Chef Dufour had said he had enough supplies to last until Tuesday. The Searles had seated themselves together and were talking in low voices. Melissa was unable to catch what they were saying and hoped that if it was important, Alasdair was picking it up with his acute hearing. She looked around the table. Just yesterday evening there had been twelve of them to dinner, and here they were Saturday lunch and there were only nine of them left. If it carried on at this rate, Chef Dufour would have supplies for a week.

She tried to get a plan for the afternoon in her head. First, the governess. Then a walk, and a final test of whether William Gauntlet could have been killed without being seen. She would need someone other than Alasdair as it would require two pairs of eyes. She sincerely hoped that Sheridan and Charles would find some way out of the estate. This gloomy, sinister old house and its corpses were getting to her. Still, their morning was enough to have given anyone the collywobbles. Two deaths in so many hours – it was incredible, fantastic, frankly unbelievable. Three, if you counted yesterday. Four if you included Lavender Gauntlet, Davinia's grandmother. What was it that had torn this family apart? Who could the murderer be?

She looked around the table at the four surviving members of the family. Could it really be one of them? She hated to think so. Was it as simple as Roderick killing his cousin and then his mother killing him in turn? That would certainly fit the facts. Would the police be satisfied with that solution, and if they were, would she be contributing to letting a murderer off scot-free? No, they would search Petunia's rooms first, then to the governess. They would have to be quick as it became dark by four o'clock and she certainly did not want to be out walking in the dark. Not here, not ever.

She squeezed Alasdair's thigh under the table. He turned towards her. 'Shall we go and start on Petunia's rooms?' she asked. Shall I ask Thomas to come too?'

'Yes. Two pairs of eyes are better than one,' Alasdair replied drily, and Melissa felt a pang of guilt, it being so close to her own thoughts, and then sympathy. He was always going to have to stand back and let others do the sighted work. But, then, look how his other senses compensated. He might never be fully happy, but he could surely embrace the life he was leading. More so than he was now? Embroiled in murder? She grinned suddenly, her mood restored. Well, it was his fault for being a spy and not telling her. He would have to take his excitement now he was blind as it came. And it certainly was coming thick and fast this weekend.

FIFTY-SIX

A short while later, Alasdair was sitting in Petunia Gauntlet's siting room listening to Melissa and Thomas rummaging around the room. He had suggested they began with her bedroom, that being, he considered, the most likely place she would store anything. This room was too accessible to the rest of the family. Her bedroom should have been more private. But he had been outvoted, he rather felt because both of them were somewhat squeamish about searching a room with the owner's dead body in it. He had no compunction. The things he had done as a spy often did not bear up to his own exacting scrutiny, but then the country had been at war, he argued with himself. However, he had to accept that this was a job that was not suited to his current particular talents. He sat stroking Sheba and tried not to feel sorry for himself.

'I can find nothing, sir.'

'Me neither, Alasdair,' Melissa added.

'You have checked through all the books, under drawers, behind drawers, under chairs?' Alasdair wanted this to be thorough. He heard some shuffling but again it was clear there was nothing.

'Come on, Thomas,' Melissa said. 'Let's be brave and try the bedroom.'

'Don't forget under the mattress.' Alasdair added with a ghoulish satisfaction. He may not be able to see, but he could certainly lead operations. 'Tell me if you find anything.'

Melissa made an odd noise in her throat and Alasdair surmised she was pulling a face at him. Suddenly, he had a foolish desire to poke his tongue out at her but resisted just in time. Senior sleuths did not descend to that level. His humour restored, he began tickling Sheba behind the ears, enjoying the thump of her tail on the carpet in response to his ministrations.

'Found something.' Melissa came very nearly straight back in. 'Blast it. You were right. It was tucked into the underside of her bedside drawer. Let's see. It is a letter addressed to Lavender Gauntlet. This must be it. Shall I fetch Thomas? I left him feeling under the mattress, not nice.'

'Oh, go on then.' Alasdair schooled himself to be patient.

'Here we are then.' There was a rustle as Melissa opened the envelope and unfolded a letter. 'Gosh, it runs to several pages. South African stamp. Clearly Lavender had written to an old friend in South Africa, looking for information about Roderick Gauntlet. Listen to this!'

Yes please, thought Alasdair at last. His patience was on a knife edge.

'Let me see … ah, here. "Lavender, dear, I have made some discreet enquiries as you requested and I am very sorry to tell you that the results have not been good. It would appear that your nephew, despite being a major in the Rifles, was a reprehensible character. It appears he was let go from the regiment and it was all hushed up. I was firmly requested to give my word that I would not repeat it to anyone other than yourself, and you know, dear, my word is my bond.

"'"He apparently was put in charge of a camp where Boers were detained, including wives and children. It looks like he pocketed money that should have been spent on food, hygiene and medicine. Made himself rich out of the suffering. Of course, there was a feeling that they were the enemy, but, my dear, I am reliably told twenty-eight thousand women and children died in the camps. Of course, it wasn't just his camp, but I am told his was the worst, exacerbated by his cheating. They never found his money, but he was not welcome in the mess again and most old soldiers and their families would have cold-shouldered him. They think he then went off into the velt after mines, I believe. The last anyone heard of him is that he was living in Cape Town persuading nuwelings off the boats to invest in projects. Of course, word got about and I think someone came after him. So he booked a passage out quick. I am very sorry to hear he is with you. He may seem charming but he is a complete skurk. Get him out of your house as soon as you can." Then she goes on about some mutual friends and just some chit chat.'

'Well, that seems to sum him up rather nicely,' Alasdair said. 'Melissa put it in your notebook safe. Now we must interview Hazel Richards. I suspect she has rather a tale to tell.'

'Indeed I do,' came the cultured voice of Hazel Richards from the doorway. She walked in and shut the door. 'The children have gone off with their mother so I am free to talk to you. It is not a nice story.'

'But you do not sound South African at all,' Melissa protested.

'My family are not Afrikaans. Well, my mother was on her mother's side, but my father was English. We are South African but Anglo. We have English heritage, but we have many friends who are Afrikaans. When the South African war started, I was the eldest. My parents sent me to family in Cape Town and then back to England to stay with some aunts. I then went to school here and did not return until I was eighteen. By then my whole family – my mother and two little brothers – had died in the camp run by Roderick Gauntlet. My father, once his supply shop was shut and then torched to stop him supplying his neighbours with food, ironically joined the army, the British army, and was killed in a skirmish.'

'Yes, Kitchener employed a scorched earth policy. I read about it. I didn't know he made the English suffer too.'

'My father had a supply shop. His customers were Afrikaans farmers. The whole town was torched, and the inhabitants moved into camps. My mother had no reason to suspect she and my brothers were in any danger going with their neighbours, the Afrikaans. And by the time the mistake was spotted by the authorities, they were dead. I've spent years researching this. You can believe me.'

'I believe you,' Alasdair said quietly. 'But what led you here?'

'I'm not sure. I wanted to look the man in the eye who could let women and children starve and die for lack of medicine. Just for money. I am not sure, maybe revenge? A little. I came after the grandmother, Lavender, died. So, I didn't know of this communication. It would have been interesting, would it not, if this had come out? His cousin William I didn't like either, but I think he would have turned Roderick out if he'd known. The honour of the regiment was all to him.'

'But if Petunia has this letter, it means she must have taken it from Lavender. Oh my giddy aunt. This means it is a motive for murder. Did she kill her twin sister?' Melissa's voice rose in appalled horror.

'Pure speculation and completely unprovable now,' Alasdair dismissed. This was all getting too dramatic for his liking.

'Trust me. You may not be able to prove it, but it was completely in character. I've lived here six months and she was a nasty old woman. But clever. I kept well away, and now I realise my instincts saved me.'

'Tell me,' Alasdair said, 'is there anyone in the family you do like?'

'The children. They are innocents. No children should suffer. And perhaps Davinia. She has a kind heart. I shall leave and return to South Africa as soon as I can. It's where I belong. Despite being a "treasure".' She laughed. 'You don't need to worry. I've done nothing wrong. Just frightened a disgusting human being a little. Do you know he wanted to pay me? He thought I was a blackmailer. Believed he could buy me off, that I could be compensated for my loss. No. I preferred to watch him drink and drink and drink. Like the dronkie he was. Do you think that was conscience?'

'Perhaps,' Alasdair said, 'but I wouldn't bank on it. Go back to South Africa, begin a new life. Forget all this.'

'Will you have enough money to be able to support yourself?' Melissa asked, perhaps remembering the nice clothes and expensive perfume.

'My father was compensated for the loss of his shop and I inherited it. I kept ownership of the land and then they discovered, under the scorched town, diamonds. I am a rich woman. Don't you fear, Mrs Charters.'

'Well then, I can only wish you luck. You must have it. For without the confession from Petunia that she killed her son, we might have thought it was you,' Alasdair said.

'Really? She did that? Well, perhaps I should've liked her after all.' Hazel Richards laughed but without humour.

FIFTY-SEVEN

'I say, you don't think that … ?' Melissa began.

'Don't even consider it,' Alasdair said firmly. 'The simplest explanation is the best.'

Melissa glanced at Thomas and caught a flash of amusement on his face that swiftly vanished. She knew he thought she was always looking for complications and conspiracies often when there were none. Sometimes there must be complications, but then why would Petunia protect Hazel Richards? Was she proud to have killed her only son? Melissa shrugged and moved on. Swiftly.

'You do realise, sir,' Thomas said, 'that from what she said, Roderick Gauntlet must have money somewhere. And quite a lot of it?'

'Yes,' Alasdair agreed, 'but that's not our concern. I will alert Sheridan. It is his bag apparently, and as he is marrying Davinia, I am sure he will pursue it to his utmost. I would be intrigued to see if Roderick Gauntlet left a will. It might be he had more to leave than his cousin.'

'But then why defraud his family?' Melissa argued, perplexed.

Thomas cast a sad expression over her. 'Because he could. Evil to the heart of him. We've met those types before, haven't we, sir?'

'Yes, and sadly I think it runs in the family. Of

course, this house doesn't help. If I was fanciful, which I am not, I would have said it was cursed. The sooner they all leave the better. And us too. So much for a pleasant sojourn in Somerset.'

Melissa looked at Alasdair in amazement, then realised she would have to put it in words. 'Well, Alasdair, you surprise me. It sounds awfully fanciful to me. But then perhaps …' She mused. 'It is one of your special skills.'

'What, soaking up atmospheres? Come on, time for that walk. We will need to bundle up. It seems to be getting colder.'

'Huh, well it is not helped that we are sitting here in the draught of an open window.' Melissa rubbed her arms. 'Let's go.'

They began by circumnavigating the house as they had yesterday morning. Melissa shivered in remembrance. So much had happened since yesterday. At least it seemed the water was receding. She popped a look in the kitchen garden and was glad to see that as it was on the same height as the house, so had not flooded. If they had to stay for another few days, they could survive on vegetables. They carried on past the back of the house and began to walk down the drive. They could hear laughter and conversation further down. Alasdair let Sheba off the lead.

'We'll let her run free. She won't go far. She has been cooped up far too much since we have been here.'

Quite a long way down the drive they found Sheridan and Charles. Melissa could clearly see the gate posts. 'Can you get any further?' she called. Both Sheridan and Charles were wearing waders.

'We were just about to try but thought we should let someone know. We don't want any more accidents,' Charles called back.

Melissa and Alasdair waited to see what happened. They were wearing gumboots but it looked like the puddles were still deep. The water was black and Melissa was worried about hidden objects.

There was a whoop of success.

'Hey, we are on the road. It is higher than the land around here so the water is definitely draining off. What do you think, Charles?'

'What, about four to six inches? I wouldn't want to risk the car but maybe tomorrow we could try it on foot.'

Charles and Sheridan began to make their way back up the drive to where Melissa and Alasdair where standing.

'Where would you go?' Alasdair asked.

'There is a village about five miles away in one direction and another about eight miles in the other. That one is bigger. It would also take us to a bridge over a river. We could then see how full it is. We could have lying water in the fields for months, but at least we could get in and out. I am trying to wrack my brains for the nearest telephone. That is the most urgent.'

'I guess it depends on where the lines are down. I assume it is that,' Alasdair suggested. 'Thomas could see nothing wrong with your phone. Wait a moment, can you see the phone wire coming from the house? Perhaps you could trace it and see if a post is down.'

Charles and Sheridan greeted this with enthusiasm and accompanied Melissa and Alasdair up the driveway. They split up at the top of the drive and Melissa, not wishing to repeat where they had been this morning, took the higher bank above the moat. As she stood there, she saw Marjorie Gauntlet standing at the drawing room window and waved.

'There is just one more way I would like to try, if you don't mind,' she said. 'Yesterday when we went on our early walk we circumnavigated the whole house. And I think that there is a high hedge from the left-hand corner of the house across to beyond the garages. Come on, let's look.'

There was indeed a high hedge screening off the servant side of the house, the outbuildings and the garage with Dunmore's quarters over the top.

'Where is Sheba?' she remarked. 'She has been gone ages.' At that moment, the dog came from the far side of the house, running past the high hedge, down the far bank behind the garages that skirted the moat and onto the lower bank and grass that was revealed from the receding flood. Then she disappeared from sight. Melissa blinked with surprise and then moved swiftly along the bank they were standing on. Sheba, wherever she had gone, was invisible to them and to the house.

She returned to Alasdair. 'Well, I'll be blowed. Sheba has shown me how William Gauntlet could have been murdered without anyone necessarily seeing it. Come on, let us move on. Can you call Sheba? We don't want to lose her.'

They went all the way along the high hedge and along to the end of the garage building, to where the moat went underground. There was a bank running down to the lower edge of the moat. The only way to access that bank was through the garages and out the other side or from Dunmore's flat. He had an exterior staircase on the outside of the building.

Melissa led Alasdair into the garages and looked for an exit. There was a door in the wall. But when she tried it, it was locked. She stood back and looked at Sheba. How had she done it? Sheba ran into the garages and barked. In the corner, obscured by a barrel, was a hole. It looked as if it had been recently dug. A fox perhaps? It was just big enough for Sheba to wriggle her way through. Melissa caught her and put her on the lead. She didn't want her disappearing again. She heard a familiar sound. In the corner of the yard was a henhouse. That explained the fox, but the hole was not big enough for a person to get through; even the children would be too big. She puzzled for a moment.

To get out that way, the murderer would have had to climb up the wooden stairs into Dunmore's flat and then out of it down the stone backstairs. Was that why Dunmore had been incapacitated? So he could not help William Gauntlet and so that he would not be able to identify the murderer?

If only Dunmore could regain consciousness and tell them. Then the murder would be solved.

She excitedly told Alasdair of her findings and he agreed that this could certainly be one explanation. Cross by his lack of enthusiasm, she had to curb her desire to stamp her foot, as she was sure she was right . . . What other explanation could there be?

FIFTY-EIGHT

Alasdair was rather amused as Melissa stomped moodily beside him. She was so happy with her solution, and it was good up until a point, but she still hadn't pinpointed the murderer. Tea was going to be interesting.

As they entered the house, Thomas was there anticipating them as usual. They changed from their gumboots into brogues and handed him their Warm coats and mufflers.

'Sir, perhaps I had better take the dog too. She is far too muddy for the drawing room.'

'Golly, Thomas, you are right.' Melissa nudged Alasdair. 'All that wriggling though holes.'

'I'll let her dry off downstairs and give her a quick brush. It's nearly time for her supper. Sir?'

'Of course, Thomas. I expect the children are down for tea today and they do so want to pet her. I think it is best if she is left alone.'

Melissa took Alasdair's arm, 'Come on, time to face the music. Or some of it at least.'

Tea was tiny egg sandwiches and he thought he smelled Marmite, too. As Alasdair bit into one he recoiled slightly in surprise, but then wolfed it down. Was Melissa laughing up her sleeve? She loved serving up surprises. Marmite was a taste that definitely should be forewarned about, though. Had it been served up especially for the children? He could hear them playing; there was a wooden clink on the floor and the children were chattering excitedly, but not loud enough to disturb the adults. Hazel Richards might have been masquerading as a governess, but she seemed to have done a good job. So good a job, he surmised, that now they were old enough to reason with, Serena might not need quite so much help. She certainly would have to do without Hazel Richards in future, he thought guiltily.

Davinia walked towards him – he could tell her footsteps and her scent. 'Hello, Davinia,' he said, as she touched his arm. She removed it quickly and he smiled at her surprise. He loved doing this; it was one small score over the rest of the world.

'Is there any news?' she asked quietly.

'Yes, but I fear it may not be suitable for small ears.' He indicated the direction in which he heard the children.

'Yes, very clever.' He could hear the smile in her voice. 'But it is not necessarily me you have to impress. I have told the family about Petunia. It is sad, but she made it hard to mourn for her.'

'Let me know when the children are gone and ask the family to remain. I can fill them in on the investigation so far.'

'Serena, can you ask Miss Richards to take the children for a short while?' Clearly Davinia did not want to wait. 'I think we need to have a meeting. Oh no, don't go,' she said. 'You don't mind if Colonel and Mrs Searle stay do you, Alasdair? For Mother,' she added quietly.

The door opened. He heard the groans from the children and assumed one of the staff must have fetched Miss Richards.

The governess must have signed to Melissa in some way, causing her to say, 'Yes, Miss Richards, we will impart your story, won't we, Alasdair? With your permission?'

She must have received an affirmative as the door closed and he heard them leave. He did wish people would speak. All this talk with nods and eye contact was extremely frustrating.

'Dobson, that is all now, thank you, we can manage from here.' The door closed again. 'And you, Elsie.' There was a giggle and again the door closed.

'So, please tell us what you know. The suspense is killing me,' Davinia urged.

'I believe it began with a letter that Lavender Gauntlet wrote to a friend in South Africa.'

'Oh, Granny. Was she murdered then?'

'Davinia, quiet, honey, let him tell the story,' Sheridan said, and Alasdair nodded his thanks in his direction, he hoped.

'Her reply contained damning information about your Uncle Roderick. To say he was evil is almost an understatement. I can only assume, as we found this letter in Petunia's possession, that either she acted on it – so yes, your grandmother may have been murdered – or she died naturally and your Great Aunt Petunia came into possession of it after she had died and before her son could destroy it. I suggest that you lean towards her not being murdered – less sensational once the police arrive. We might also think about just how much of this we want to share.'

'But it'll be needed to provide motive, won't it?' Sheridan said.

'Well, I personally think far more of a motive was

that Petunia discovered that her son not only had fleeced herself of her money but was also actively doing the same to the rest of the family. I think money is a far more likely candidate for motive.'

'Why did he do that?' Charles said.

'I suspect because he could. I need to inform you that he was not poor when he arrived here. If you ask her nicely, I think Hazel Richards will be able to enlighten you further.'

Alasdair then proceeded to give them a résumé of her story. 'I imagine, Sheridan, if you search hard enough you will find the money. Of course, if he has invested in Bernard Lyons, it will surely be lost. The family should also try to find a will, if Roderick made one, as they could have a claim as next of kin. Especially now his mother is dead.'

Melissa looked around the room. Everyone was rather dazed. No one even asked questions; they just sat there as if in shock. She rang the servant bell and, when Dobson appeared at the door, ordered brandy, whisky and glasses. Purely for medicinal purposes, of course.

'What about William? Did she kill him too?' Marjorie asked in a quavering voice.

'To be frank, we don't know. I have an idea about it,' Alasdair added, 'but it is not something I can pursue at the moment. Unless there is anything any of you want to tell me? I suggest we all disperse and have a think. Assuming Charles and Sheridan can get to civilisation tomorrow, we need to prepare for the police. I think it is very unlikely that they will leave it to the local constable. It will be the county police at the very least.

'You will also need to fetch the doctor, for death

certificates or post-mortems may be needed. Nurse Foote is excellent but doctors tend to have their own ideas. I also suggest you contact your family lawyer and get him here as soon as possible. Oh and one last thing – on no account is the room of Roderick Gauntlet to be disturbed. Even if you do want to chase the money, it will have to wait. It is his death that could be the sticking point, and any evidence of rifling the room will be viewed as very suspicious by the police.'

FIFTY-NINE

Alasdair lifted up the glass of his watch and felt for the time. It was five thirty. Thomas was outside in the hall with Sheba. He handed Alasdair the lead and enquired whether they would need help dressing. He added that the meal tonight would be stew. Did he think it was necessary to dress for dinner?

'Always,' Alasdair replied gloomily. 'But don't worry, I am sure I can ask Melissa to help.' He took her hand in his and smiled at her.

'No, sir, I'll pop up at six and lay things out and draw your bath, don't you worry.'

'Very well, Thomas,' Alasdair conceded. Unbeknownst to him, both Thomas and Melissa exchanged relieved glances.

'Best not to change anything now. With any luck we may be able to leave tomorrow or Tuesday at the latest. Let's go and hide in our room. Any chance of more tea, Thomas?'

'I'll bring it up shortly, madam.' Thomas's voice was warm; order had been restored.

They sat either side of the small table in their room, sipping tea and dunking biscuits and discussing the case. Melissa was exhausted and was having to work hard not to be snappy. Much as she had liked Davinia, she had to admit to herself that her family were rather ghastly and could not wait to leave. It was such a shame she had come down here with such hope and enthusiasm. Just a little problem to solve and what had they? Three dead bodies and a fourth soon, if Nurse Foote was to be relied on. She rubbed her eyes. 'Sorry, Alasdair, what were you saying?'

'Darling, you are tired. Come on, let's rest. We can just nip under the eiderdown. Thomas can wake us when he comes to prepare for dinner.'

'I wonder what I should wear?' Melissa yawned and fell into a deep sleep, only awaking when Thomas began pouring the bath, which seemed a short while later. She thanked the heavens that she had, at the last moment, packed a burgundy velvet dress. It was a little short for mourning wear but she hoped the colour was sombre enough to set the right tone. She just could not face wearing the same black dress yet again. She looked with longing at the royal blue silk flapper dress still hanging in the wardrobe, with its delightful handkerchief hem, but knew it would not be worn on this trip.

Bathed and ready, having still not discussed the case in any detail, they went down the stairs. Melissa had put on a bright red lipstick to lift the colour in her face, and she felt the fillip of strength such flimsy armour gave her.

They were the last to enter the drawing room. Nurse Foote and Miss Richards were not in attendance. Davinia came over and said it would just be nine for dinner this evening. 'We wanted to keep it small and intimate, limited to the family, yourselves and the Searles included, of course. We have asked the servants to keep things minimal this evening.'

That did not apply to the alcohol, Melissa noted,

as Dobson handed them both champagne in glasses. No sherry this evening. To Melissa's raised eyebrows, Davinia added, rather defensively, 'Well, I wanted to celebrate my engagement. It rather fell flat yesterday evening. Please do not stint yourselves. Dobson says there is plenty in the cellar.'

Melissa sipped the bubbling nectar – it was good champagne, from a beautiful etched glass coupe – and raised her glass to Davinia. Now was not the time to quibble over proprieties. It was 1923, after all. 'To you, Davinia, may you be happy.'

Charles tapped his signet ring against the side of his glass. 'To the future Mr and Mrs Kennard.' He raised his glass. 'May their future be happy and full.'

Everyone raised their glasses, and faint 'Hear hears' could be heard about the room.

The fire popped and crackled in the large fireplace, the glow sending waves of warmth into the room. The standard lamps all about the room were lit and the few remaining bronzes glinted in the light. The sheen of the flock on the claret-coloured wallpaper dappled. Looking around the room and absorbing this moment of celebration, the glasses full of bubbly shining, Melissa could almost imagine this barn of a room as cosy. Almost, but not quite. She shivered and was grateful for the knitted evening bolero she had slipped on.

'Come on then, let us go into dinner. We have much to discuss. With the door firmly shut, we should be able to talk in private.' Charles was assuming command.

'I am afraid the meal will be a bit of a hotchpotch this evening,' said Davinia. 'By tomorrow we will be eating out of tins if we cannot get more supplies.'

'You may have to sacrifice a few of your chickens.' Charles grinned, but Melissa thought he was not completely joking.

However, she had no complaints with the hearty vegetable soup that was the first course. Instead of a fish course, they had a small pot of something au gratin, which Melissa did not recognise. It was delicious and aniseed flavoured.

'Gosh, what is this?' Melissa asked. 'It is wonderful.'

'Fennel,' Davinia enlightened her. 'Chef Dufour grows it in the kitchen garden.'

'Well, I must make a note of it, and we must grow it too. It is blissful.'

The main course was heavenly: buttery mashed potatoes with parsnip and cream to accompany a rich, dark beef stew with mushrooms. It was then that Melissa just knew she would have to sponsor Chef Dufour's restaurant – and hopefully somewhere near to where they lived.

As soon as Dobson and Thomas had left after serving this course, Charles said, 'Now we can begin to discuss our futures.'

'Well,' began Marjorie, 'I am still going to leave and live in Charmouth. I shall be leaving just as soon as I can with Elizabeth and Arthur. They have invited me to stay for a while and I shall look for something to rent. Apparently in the winter there are lots of properties available.'

Davinia looked around the table and said, 'Well, we have celebrated my news. Sheridan and I will be getting married as soon as we can, but Sheridan still has some other leads he needs to follow up over here. As soon as he has collected enough evidence, we shall return to the States and report back.'

'Do you think you will have enough information to stop Bernard Lyons trading in the United States?' Alasdair asked.

'I certainly have enough to show he is unscrupulous and sails very close to the wind, but then that is almost the American way.' Sheridan smiled. 'However, unless it is enough to prove actual fraud, I don't know. Perhaps. Certainly enough to put the word out in financial quarters to make it hard for him to make big enough killings to stay on. But if he has made himself unpopular here, in South Africa and then the US, he is going to run out of world pretty quickly.'

Alasdair thought he sounded far too confident for his own good. When did enough money become more than enough? More than enough to settle down to a quiet comfortable life? Bernard Lyons had appeared not to have settled for that quite yet, but if he did, Alasdair felt sure it would be very difficult to expose him for the man he truly was. A man with money could be despised and admired in turn.

'Well, Serena and I have discussed things,' said Charles, 'and I am going to give her father's offer a go. See if I have what it takes to go into trade and learn the business from him. In which case, we too do not want to stay in this place. We will move closer to her parents in Devon. We would like to be near the sea.'

'What does that mean then?' Marjorie quavered.

'As soon as I can find a phone, I will set our lawyer into action. Assuming the will is correct, we will all have money. Not quite as much as we thought but enough.

Thank you, Alasdair, for offering us hope with Roderick Gauntlet. Sheridan, I hope you can help with tracking down his finances.'

'I'll do what I can,' the American responded, with a dip of his head.

'So, am I surmising,' Alasdair said, 'that you all feel the case is closed?'

'Well, it must be,' Charles Gauntlet replied. 'We can show that Great Aunt Petunia killed Uncle Roderick, and then she died from natural causes.'

'But what of your father? How will you explain that away?'

'Well, perhaps it was an accident after all?'

'You will need to convince a doctor of that and persuade Nurse Foote that she was mistaken. Not an easy task.'

'Well, if that is the case' – Serena spoke for the first time – 'could it not be argued that Roderick Gauntlet killed his cousin? If he was such a rotter, isn't that the likeliest solution? It was, after all, what we were all thinking.' She glanced up and down the table to small nods.

'But,' Alasdair remonstrated, 'you are going to have to deal with the police and—'

The door opened and Nurse Foote stood there a moment before she stumbled in, sat on the first vacant chair, covered her face and began to cry. Between sobs, she managed, 'Frank Dunmore is dead.'

SIXTY

Melissa rushed across to her and knelt before her and took her hand. 'Poor Nurse Foote. This has been a terrible strain for you, hasn't it? What a calamity, all these deaths.'

'I have been so wicked, wicked.' The nurse had taken out a handkerchief and was mopping her face and eyes.

'What do you mean, Nurse Foote?' Alasdair had risen and was walking towards them. Melissa took his hand and guided it to the back of the chair that Nurse Foote was sitting in.

'You knew, didn't you, Mr Charters? I thought you suspected. You are far too canny. Too knowing of human nature. That's why I tried to keep you with me.'

'And tried to stop me questioning Petunia. You are a kind woman, a caring woman, and you felt that William Gauntlet deserved his fate. His actions resulted in the death of the man you loved.'

'Good gad, is there no end to the infamy of those two cousins?' Captain Searle exclaimed. 'I am sorry, Marjorie, but you married into a rotten family.'

'But created a very lovely one in Davinia and Charles and his children,' Elizabeth, his wife, chided him, no doubt trying to soften his harsh outburst. 'It is to the new generations we must look. They have the opportunity to create something good.'

'You're right.' Nurse Foote sat up higher. 'That's why

what I did was wicked. I wanted you to be punished. So many others had suffered hereabouts after the tribunals William Gauntlet sat on. But now I see that he made you all suffer. Especially you, Mrs Gauntlet' – she turned to Marjorie – 'with your pills and potions and nerves. It was your escape, wasn't it?'

Marjorie Gauntlet began to cry, and Elizabeth Searle put an arm about her for comfort.

'You see,' Nurse Foote continued, 'I had in my hand the means to make you all suffer. If the police'd come, I would have said something earlier. If anyone'd been charged with murder I'd have confessed. But then we were trapped here, and once I'd started it, I couldn't stop. William Gauntlet deserved to suffer . . . '

'I think being hit on the head and then held under water until he drowned was suffering enough, don't you think?' Alasdair replied drily. No one present could think they were let off the hook.

'Always at the heart of the matter.' Nurse Foote sounded bitter. She pulled a letter out of her pocket. 'I knew he were unlikely to survive, but I didn't want him to do so and then hang. It is all in there. It were in his pocket. So I waited, but he took so long to die.' She began to sob again.

Melissa took the letter.

'What is it?' Alasdair asked, frustration making him snap. He returned to his place at the table, his temper making him fumble with pulling the chair out.

'A letter from Dunmore,' Melissa exclaimed.

'Another letter. This case is beset by letters. Does no one talk any more?' he exploded, then forced himself to remain calm; after all, it was not their fault he was blind.

This was just his own frustration. 'What does it say? Just the gist will do for now,' he added quietly.

Melissa scanned the letter. 'It is a bit rambling. I think he must have been drunk when he wrote it. Here, um, he had an argument with the Colonel last night. He wanted him to clear the moat. Oh dear, yes, not good.' She looked up and saw the entire room agog. 'Frank Dunmore had a brother. He too had weak lungs, but William Gauntlet passed him fit all the same. He died. Apparently when Dunmore refused to work on the moat, the Colonel said, and I quote, "Showing lack of moral fibre just like your weedy little brother. Well I saw to him, and I'll see to you too." Gosh, it looks like Dunmore spent all night getting drunk and working himself up.' She shuffled several pages. 'Oh, here it is. "I have done it. That's avenged Tim. I wonder how he liked suffering, having his lungs filled up and drowning in muck. Time to join my brother. Good job I pocketed the old woman's powders. I can sleep now and meet Tim on the other side with my head held high."'

'Thank you, Melissa. Keep it safe with the other evidence,' Alasdair began, then frowned. 'What is that noise?' he called, raising his voice. The hubbub of background conversation in the room died. And there it was: the high-pitched trilling of the telephone.

It stopped and Dobson entered the room. 'Apparently the lines are now working, ladies and gentlemen. It seems Nurse Foote is sorely missed and can they send transport for her first thing in the morning?'

SIXTY-ONE

As a non sequitur, it was a classic. Melissa watched the amazement spreading across the faces of those still at the table. Alasdair just put his head in his hands. his shoulders shaking. She then realised he was guffawing with laughter. It was infectious and they all began to chuckle in response, some of it tinged with more than a little hysteria.

Melissa folded up the letter and placed it carefully in the envelope and then into her notebook that she had carried down in her suitably large beaded and embroidered evening bag which her Aunt Honor had lovingly made for her. Also nestled in the bottom was her little pea shooter, just in case.

'Come, Nurse Foote, you have had a rotten time of it.' Davinia took charge. 'Come upstairs and we will draw you a bath. I can find something for you to change into. Serena, ring the bell. Elsie can wash your uniform. What you need now is a good night's sleep. We can sort everything out in the morning.'

Melissa wondered if it would be as easy as all that, or whether Nurse Foote would have regained her equilibrium and sense of justice in the morning – and just what would she say to the doctor and the police?

She returned to the table and sat next to Alasdair, but not before she had swiped a nearly full bottle of champagne from an ice bucket on the side and refilled both their glasses.

Alasdair shook his head at her but then shrugged and took a swig. 'So now we must decide how to play this. Did Dunmore have any other family?'

'Dunmore?' Charles was clearly being slow, still focused on himself, no doubt.

'Well, I am thinking of any complications there might be and Nurse Foote's sensibilities. She is actually a very moral person. She certainly protected your Great Aunt Petunia's interests when she felt she needed them. Think, man, we all need to present a united front to the police.' He paused. 'Now, Charles, I suggest you phone Dr Haymes, is it? Tell him you have four dead bodies in the house, one of them potentially suspicious, two suicides and one natural causes. Once he has picked himself off of the floor, you can leave the rest to him. I suspect he will phone the county police. Once we know whom we are dealing with, I can phone contacts in London to help smooth the way if necessary.

'Miss Richards will not be a problem. She has her own reasons for keeping quiet and I imagine will book the first ship to South Africa available. Let her go, she is a complication we can do without.' He added, 'Charles, go and telephone now before the switchboard girl goes off to bed. And keep it succinct. I assume it is a she?'

There were nods, then Charles said, 'Yes, postmistress, village shop, switchboard.'

'Yes. Assume she will be listening in. Keep calm and to the point. Go. Go!' Alasdair took another swig of champagne. 'Just let me think while he is gone.' Everyone fell silent. If Alasdair sensed all the remaining eyes on the room focused on him, he ignored them. He had closed his eyes and rested his head on one hand, the other hand on the table. His fingertips were beating a tattoo on the tablecloth.

The door clicked as Charles came back, 'Well for once Dr Haymes was in. He will be here at nine o'clock tomorrow morning. He is phoning the Police Divisional Headquarters now and fully expects someone to join him from there tomorrow morning. He will phone back if there are any difficulties.'

'How are the roads then? Will they be able to get here?' Melissa asked anxiously.

'Apparently the bridge held and although there was much localised flooding like here, the main roads are now clear. So they should get fairly close to us even if they have to walk the last part of the way,' Charles said.

'It hasn't started raining again, so the floods here may have receded even more by tomorrow,' Sheridan added. 'Perhaps we could get out early and clear the rest of the drive and check the low road tomorrow? Whaddya say, Charles?'

'Make sure you do it together,' Alasdair said drily. 'We do not need any more accidents.'

SIXTY-TWO

The door opened and Davinia slipped in. 'I have popped Nurse Foote into bed. She has had a plate of sandwiches and a hot drink. She is exhausted. Frankly I think it is amazing that she is still upright. Elsie will stay with her until she is asleep, just in case she needs anything.'

'Did she say anything about her revelations?' Charles sounded frightened.

'She does not want a fuss made. Dunmore has paid for his crime and cannot be held accountable now. She will agree to any version of events that we present to the police.'

'So, may I suggest that you, Alasdair, and you, Melissa, present the case as you see it to the police tomorrow? I think it would help if we were not seen to be too keen as a family to offer explanations. Don't you?' Charles continued.

'I agree,' Alasdair said. 'You will, of course, all face quite intense questioning from the police. May I suggest the following line of replies? The least damning line of enquiry is yours, Sheridan. I assume you can present your credentials?'

'Yeah, no problem. It would be a great kindness to the family if all mention of the tribunals, South Africa and anything else of that nature could be kept quiet. Not hushed up, you understand, just not mentioned if at all possible.'

'Yes, especially if Charles is to go into business in the area.' Alasdair said, 'For the sake of your children, I agree. Right, Dunmore must have killed Colonel Gauntlet in a drunken rage, then in remorse killed himself. We will have to give the police the letter, but I think we could ask them to be subtle over the reasoning behind the killings. They may be sensitive. We shall have to see. Nurse Foote said most of the local people know about the tribunals and the role Colonel Gauntlet had in them. You may have to take that one on the chin. It might help' – he turned towards Marjorie Gauntlet – 'if you showed proper horror at what was done by your husband and the family were equally contrite.'

'Of course, we are contrite, damn it,' Charles muttered. 'Sometimes I think he was a monster. But a monster that once he got his own way could be generous and kind.' He gave a sob, tears running down his face. 'Robert and Lucy will at least remember a grandfather with affection.'

A wry smile played over Alasdair's lips. It was not how he would have wanted to bring his children up, but all families were different. 'Charles, you will sell this house then?'

'Oh yes, we cannot stay here. Not that it will fetch much. Who on earth would want to live here after all this death?'

'You would be surprised,' Alasdair muttered. 'Should you contact your lawyer as well? You are clear on the sequence of events? Dunmore killed Colonel Gauntlet. You then discovered that his cousin Roderick Gauntlet had been defrauding the family, and his mother Petunia in fury killed her son with his own revolver. Will that wash, do you think?'

'Yes, I think that is a very sensible solution. The simpler the better,' Arthur Searle, agreed. 'You can count on Elizabeth and I to be discreet.'

'It seems I will have a never-ending debt of thank-you to you all.' Charles, for once, sounded humble.

'We will all have to give it. Come, I will ring the bell and get Dobson to serve dessert and coffees in here. You can have the port with ladies present for once, can you not?' Davinia sounded at her most appealing. The table readily assented, and dinner resumed as if the house did not possess four dead.

SIXTY-THREE

The following morning Doctor Haymes arrived promptly, as did an ambulance. The police came in two cars: a superintendent and an inspector with two constables. They listened to Alasdair's explanation with something like incredulity. The inspector telephoned the Whitehall number Alasdair gave him and then, after a brief aside, their attitude was slightly more respectful, but dubious all the same. Melissa had wisely left all the talking to the men. No mention was made of Lavender Gauntlet or the reason that Alasdair and Melissa had been invited to stay.

They joined the family in the drawing room and waited … and waited and waited. Over an hour later, a rather queasy-looking Superintendent Farmer entered the room.

'Doctor Haymes has confirmed as much as he can, that your description of events concurs with the bodies he has examined. He has spoken to Nurse Foote, who has provided us with relevant details that affirms your version of events. The family solicitor is here. Apparently he has heard the news of your father, Major Charters, and seems to think that even though he does not know you personally, you would be above reproach.' He made it sound more of an accusation than a reference. Alasdair wisely did not respond.

'Dr Haymes having completed his examination, we

have authorised the removal of the bodies. He will be taking Nurse Foote with him when he goes shortly. She is needed elsewhere apparently. I must ask everyone else to remain here until we have had a chance to take statements. We will be using the study for this purpose. I have asked the governess to bring your children here. It seems she is very keen to leave, hardly surprising considering the circumstances. I will begin with her statement and she can have a lift into Taunton with the ambulance. I have told her, as I am telling you, that you will have to remain available for the inquest, which will be next week sometime.'

'That should not be a problem, Superintendent.' Charles was all graciousness. 'Can I beg a small favour? My mother is not a well woman, and this situation, especially the death of my father, has taken its toll on her. I wonder if she might be permitted to leave with our friends the Searles?' He pointed towards the three of them sitting on a sofa.

'Very well. Are you going far?' He spun round and eyed Captain Searle with some suspicion, it seemed to Melissa, but perhaps that was his natural way. She was rather disappointed at the way things were going. At this rate it looked like they would be staying another night. She crossed her fingers under cover of her handbag. She, frankly, was equally desperate to leave. She certainly felt they owed no more to Davinia, and it was very unlikely they would need any comforting in their appearance of grief. She noticed that the entire family had appeared in black this morning, and it wasn't hard to look wan in the harshness of unrelieved mourning.

'Charmouth,' Captain Searle returned with dignity,

gaining the assent he expected. 'I shall, with your permission, bring the car around and when we are packed, we can go?'

Melissa had not bothered about the other car in the garage or wondered at its ownership. Lucky them; they would soon have their escape.

It was a long, slow morning. Trapped as they were in the drawing room, a constable at the door to clearly prevent escape, those remaining were left to their own devices. Serena was sitting on the floor keeping a watchful eye on her children. A train set had been found and Robert was happily playing with it and allowing his younger sister to join in. Then Sheridan Kennard was called. Followed by Davinia, Charles, Serena and the children in turn. So there was just Alasdair and Melissa left. She held his hand stroking the top of it with her thumb. Several times she opened her mouth to say something but each time Alasdair raised a finger to his lips and pointed at the closed door.

At last it was their turn, and surprisingly they were allowed to enter the study together with Sheba leading the way. Superintendent Farmer appeared almost jovial now; the inspector was sitting beside him reviewing his notes in his own small notebook. The superintendent passed Melissa's carefully edited notebook back to her. 'Some interesting omissions in your accounts.' His eyes glittered. 'I have followed your lead and removed the relevant pages needed for our investigation. I suspect you will have to acquire a new one as the pages that have been so liberally removed have destroyed the binding.'

Melissa reached across and took hold of the notebook, smiling and looking, she hoped, suitably chastened and innocent.

'However, a word of advice to you both. It is not wise to get quite so mixed up in murders. You could gain yourselves a possibly unwelcome reputation.' He chose to ignore the grateful slump of Melissa's shoulders. Alasdair, of course, still sat ramrod straight. 'These county families can be a nest of vipers. I blame interbreeding. Fancy a pair of twins marrying another pair of twins. Not natural that is,' he continued. 'But that said, I think here the outcome will suit all concerned. I see no need to inflame the scurrilous local gossips or the press.

'We will direct a straightforward inquest. I think it unlikely there will be a need for you to attend. Given the length of journey required. Your man, Thomas, seems to have your things in order and I understand difficulties with a dog.' He peered over the desk. Sheba ignored him. 'Given that the chauffeur is dead, I have instructed Constable Whitlock to drive you all to Taunton. You should be able to pick up a train home there. He can come back should it be necessary with extra support. We will be conducting our investigation for quite a time yet.'

The inspector rose and opened the door for them. The superintendent shook both their hands and made it clear they were dismissed.

Thomas was standing in the hall with the luggage and their outdoor coats and hats, along with Davinia.

'I rather feel we are surplus to requirements.' Alasdair smiled. 'Good luck, Davinia.' He held out his hand but Davinia pulled him towards her and gave him a brief peck on the cheek. She enveloped Melissa in an extravagant hug and whispered in her ear, 'I will be in touch soon. Thank you for everything.'

Just as they were about to step into the police car, Charles appeared with a large newspaper-wrapped package and handed it to Melissa. She staggered a little under its weight. 'A little souvenir of the weekend. You did admire them. It is a dancing Kali. The goddess of death, oh, and creation.' He laughed and turned away. 'Thank you,' he called back.

THE END

ACKNOWLEDGEMENTS

Once again, I would like to thank Consuelo Rivera-Fuentes and Victorina Press for having the confidence to publish this second book.

I would like to thank Vanessa Goldie for her eagle-eyed copy-editing and advice.

A special thank you to author Judy Hall who edited the book and offered reams of advice. It is a better book because of her input. I am grateful to Katherine Trail, who did the final copy-editing on behalf of Victorina Press.

I would like to thank Bournemouth Libraries once again where I found the excellent book No Thankful Village: The Impact of the Great War on a Group of Somerset Villages – A Microcosm by Chris Howell (Fickle Hill, 3 Aug 2002). This provided the genesis of the story and is well worth a read for the first-hand accounts of those affected by the Great War.

To the Langford at Fivehead, a very comfortable fifteenth-century manor house in the heart of the Somerset Levels, where we stayed for a great weekend and soaked in the atmosphere.

ABOUT THE AUTHOR

Vicki lives in Poole Dorset with her blind physiotherapist husband. She has a lifelong fascination with the Art Deco period and with books of the Golden Age of Crime. This led her to envision a series featuring a blind detective set in the 1920s. Blind Pool is the second in the series.

Before she retired she worked as a librarian for the RNIB and for Bournemouth and Poole Public Libraries. Whilst her children were young she taught yoga during school hours. She now is busy writing and helping her husband and son in running their Physiotherapy practice.

She is a co-pioneer for a reading charity Read Easy Bournemouth and volunteers at The Russell Cotes

Museum in Bournemouth.

She is currently writing book three in the series Blind Haven set in Bournemouth.

Find her on **www.vickigoldie.com**

Subscribe to her news letter on
vickigoldie.author@gmail.com

Find her on Facebook, **Vicki Goldie Writer**

And look at her inspiration boards for her novels on Pinterest. *Blind Witness, Blind Pool,* and *Blind Haven.*

Vicki is a member of the Crime Writers Association and the Society of Authors.